ANDRE GONZALEZ

Insanity

First published by Andre Gonzalez in 2017

Copyright © Andre Gonzalez, 2017

First Edition

ISBN: 9780997754841

This book was professionally typeset on Reedsy.
Find out more at reedsy.com

Also by Andre Gonzalez

The Burden (Insanity #2) – Coming Summer 2018
A Poisoned Mind – free at www.andregonzalez.net
Followed Home – available on Amazon and BN.com

This is dedicated to anyone that has had their life forever changed by a mass shooting. As a survivor of the Aurora movie theater shooting, I found much therapy in writing this book as a way to let out the fear and tension that can be held in after such tragedy. Let us always remember those lives lost for no reason.

"So when you find yourself locked onto an unpleasant train of thought, heading for the places in your past where the screaming is unbearable, remember there's always madness. Madness is the emergency exit." -The Joker, *Batman: The Killing Joke*

1

Prologue

March 11th, 2016. 8 p.m.

The prior twelve hours had passed in a blur for Jeremy Heston. All he could remember was blood everywhere, even on the pale skin of his arm. He could hear the TV in the other room describing the scene he had left behind.

He woke with no idea what time it was or how long he had been asleep. His ride to the police station felt like years ago; in fact, it had only been ten hours. He was in a cell with blank gray walls and no window, a stiff cot and steel toilet. A barred door provided the only glimpse to the outside world, and he could see an officer sitting at a messy desk, glued to the TV.

Jeremy lay on his cot, staring dully at the ceiling, the brown waves of his grown-out hair serving as his only pillow. His usual brown eyes bulged from his sockets, but with a tint of red spread about, making him think his sleep was nowhere near the quality he preferred. Some dipshit reporter kept saying his name, along with some astronomical numbers that couldn't be right.

It needed to happen. So many more will be saved if this all goes right. He recalled a vague memory of arriving at the police station. He'd never forget the way the sun beat down on him just before they pulled him into the station, not knowing if he would ever see it again as a free man. His body ached all over, and he lifted his blood-splattered shirt to see a nasty bruise starting to form in his right armpit from the rapid firing of his rifle. *Feels like Mohammed fucking Ali punched me a few dozen times.*

He drifted, as if in and out of a cloud. A carousel of police officers stopped by his cell, some to see Jeremy and some to change their uniforms in the nearby locker room. A few were drenched in blood from head to toe.

Only one officer spoke to Jeremy, a stocky Mexican man with a thick scar across his cheek, which would be forever burned into Jeremy's memory.

He had walked out of the locker room, and as he passed by Jeremy he said, "You're gonna rot in hell for this, you piece of shit." The cop's face quivered as he spoke.

Jeremy noticed the officer's severe limp as he hobbled away like a penguin, barking at some other cops to "Get the fucking press out of here!"

Suddenly memories from Jeremy's childhood rushed his mind in a blur, but everything was covered in blood, all that goddamn blood. Even with all his planning, he forgot to anticipate the blood.

As he lay on his cot, staring at the buzzing lights on the ceiling, his mind felt clear for the first time in months. He felt in control—and, actually, relieved. The experiment was officially live and there was no turning back. Months had gone into his preparation and now the show would start.

I'm a step ahead of the game, he thought. *It's like having the answers for a test the night before.*

He knew the jury would be so appalled, they would have no choice but to call him a lunatic.

He couldn't help but smile as the tight grasp of sleep took hold of him. All the sound around him, all the commotion and shuffling footsteps, was nothing but white noise. It gave him an odd sense of comfort.

Everything will be okay.

November 2008

Jeremy's story started at Bears Field, home of the Denver Bears Baseball Club, not on the field but in the team's call center. Jeremy started his tenure with the Bears answering phones. It had come as a shock that the call center was not in the elegant front office, but tucked in the back corner, hidden from society. There were no fancy tables, no lounge chairs, no flat-screen TVs, not even any windows to see the light of day.

Behind the rows of desks, the manager's office was elevated above the floor, enclosed with glass walls so that they could keep an eye on the worker bees. *All this for a position that barely paid enough to keep the lights on.*

The room was a crescent shape, allowing all sound to carry into the manager's office, often prompting employees to send a text message to their desk neighbor instead of speaking out loud.

The job was Jeremy's first exposure to corporate shenanigans. With no experience at the ripe age of eighteen, he entered with the simple intention of trying to befriend everyone. No bad blood meant no one would fuck you over later. Ambitious for a kid out of high school—some would say naïve—but he knew that he wanted to work as a psychologist in professional sports and thought the best way to achieve it would be to get everyone on his side.

The turnover rate was high, so Jeremy saw many people come and leave the call center, mostly a mixture of retirees looking for free baseball tickets and college students looking for a flexible schedule. And free baseball tickets.

Despite the revolving door of new faces every month, friendships developed, even some that would stand the test of time, lasting long after the call center vanished from his rearview mirror.

Lewis Hamilton connected with Jeremy the instant they met. At sixty-eight, Lewis was one of the retirees working for free tickets (and a Major League Baseball pension he liked to brag about). Their friendship seemed unlikely: Lewis was a sassy old black man and Jeremy was a teenager who grew up in a middle-class suburb of Denver. But they found common ground in sports, politics, and their overall outlook on life.

Even though he wouldn't be able to legally enter a casino for three more years, Lewis took Jeremy to some casual poker games hosted at local bars; Lewis helped him get into the bars, usually having some sort of connection. The two planned to go to Las Vegas for his twenty-first birthday.

"Poker, alcohol, and women," Lewis said. "That's all you need in life, and Vegas has all three."

They played and watched poker on TV together, always wanting to learn how to perfect the craft of the game.

"People that think this is a game of luck should be taken out back and shot," Jeremy said, and Lewis agreed.

"But you can't shoot them—they're the best ones to play against. Let them sit there and wait to get lucky," Lewis said, and they laughed.

5

They played heads-up for hours, discussing life and current events. In his almost seventy years of life, Lewis had accumulated quite the vault of stories. Jeremy learned over time that if you worked in the call center long enough, you would learn Lewis's stories to the point of being able to tell them yourself. He was like a parrot thirsting for new people to talk to, to share his stories with.

As the friendship grew, so did their hunger for the poker tables. By the time he turned twenty Jeremy had won multiple bar games, which mainly paid out in free bar tabs that he gifted to Lewis. At the virtual felts online, he could play for actual money. His obsession swelled as he played online tournaments every night. He started with a twenty-dollar deposit and turned it into two hundred by the end of the first week.

The Bears had a policy that prevented part-time employees from working more than 1,200 hours within a calendar year, to avoid providing health benefits; the Harvey brothers *loved* to take care of their staff. The working-hours restriction meant that every call center employee lived below the poverty line. This didn't present as big of a problem for the retirees like Lewis as it did for the college students trying to make an actual living.

Baseball tickets couldn't pay the rent, but poker could. Jeremy enjoyed a heater of a month of June, winning more than four thousand dollars thanks to a couple of online tournament victories. He stashed the money in savings to cover rent for the next six months, leaving his paychecks to be used for entertainment—and more poker, of course.

He had read about kids his age that had dropped out of college to pursue a career in poker, traveling the world to play in different circuits. The thought crossed his mind, but worry about what his family would say swayed him to keeping the cards as a side gig. Life as a professional gambler would have to wait.

For the next year, he shifted his focus to school and tried to work his way up the ladder with the Bears. He was busy with classes three days a week, homework every night, and work every other day.

On top of that, Jeremy couldn't resist a game: he attended seventy out of the eighty home games his first season. With a paycheck that vanished into rent and food, his budget left no room for entertainment besides the free games. He lived at Bears Field that first year, rotating through friends and family to join him at the games. Once word got out, Jeremy discovered he had more "friends" than he realized. People usually bought him dinner as a thank you. *Free baseball and food, I was living like a king.*

His year-end review rolled around. "We're very impressed with your performance this season," his manager, Sammy, told him from across his desk.

His review was the first time he had sat down in the fishbowl office with the doors closed. The room had a musty smell, like old newspapers collected over decades. The tile of its elevated floor had stains and scuffs as old as the stadium.

"We love your passion, and I personally am grateful to have you as a resource for the rest of the team," Sammy continued.

Jeremy never could get a good read on Sammy, though he seemed like a decent man with good intentions for his employees. Some days he came in groggy and everyone knew to stay out of his way. Other days, his clothes looked wrinkled, his pants too tight, his hair a mess. But he kept his chin up, and Jeremy respected him for that.

"What do I need to do to move up in the organization?" Jeremy asked.

"The best thing you can do is talk to different people," Sammy responded. "At the end of the day it's about who you know."

Jeremy mulled this over, realizing he'd rarely spoken to anyone outside of the ticketing department. His goal of becoming the team's psychologist would take some ass-kissing, starting with the club's general manager, Christopher Dowd.

"How'd it go?" Lewis whispered when Jeremy returned to his desk. They had recently been assigned desks next to each other.

Jeremy grinned and gave a thumbs-up, knowing Sammy could hear everything. He returned to his homework, which he worked on between calls. In his Psych class they were discussing mental illness, a topic that interested Jeremy as he had a family member that suffered from schizophrenia.

His father never spoke of Jeremy's great-grandfather, who had been locked up in an insane asylum in the early 1900s. Jeremy knew he had killed someone, and then claimed to be an English spy sent to the United States on a mission to destroy any possible threats to England. Great Grandpa Heston had never even visited England, and doctors diagnosed him as a paranoid schizophrenic. The family had disowned poor old Louis Heston and left him to rot away the rest of his years in a small padded room.

Jeremy was well aware of the general disconnection that plagued his entire family and couldn't help but wonder if his great-grandfather's disease had some sort of shaming effect on those that followed. At the very least, he hoped to gain a better understanding of the disease from his many psychology courses planned for the next four years.

3

ctober 2009

O A year later, Jeremy finally had his much-anticipated meeting with Chris Dowd. The busy general manager had set aside a half hour to chat with Jeremy, inviting him up to his office. Jeremy had never ventured up to the second floor, where the big wigs had their offices.

Jeremy made his way up the rounded staircase, leaving his world behind to explore what he hoped would one day be his future home. The hustle and bustle of the first-floor sales and marketing teams gave way to a silent second floor. Scouts, analysts, and vice presidents with their assistants filled the space ahead of him. Walking up the stairs felt like getting called up to the big leagues.

The first desk at the top of the stairs belonged to Amelia Armstrong, Chris's assistant. She shot Jeremy a quick glance over her thick-framed glasses before returning to her computer screen.

"Jeremy?" she asked, without waiting for an answer. "Please have a seat and Mr. Dowd will be with you shortly."

"Thank you," Jeremy said, sitting in one of the chairs adjacent to her desk.

It was an unwritten rule that full-timers never spoke to, or even acknowledged, part-timers. The second floor proved no different. No one even looked in his direction. Perhaps his khakis and polo shirt made him stand out in the sea of suits. Perhaps people on the second floor were just assholes.

Amelia continued to look busy. She pursed her bright red lips together while her flat bangs pressed on her forehead. "Mr. Dowd is ready for you," she said, refusing eye contact.

Jeremy stood, hiding the tremble in his hands by putting them in his pocket. There were only thirty active Major League Baseball general managers in the world, and he was about to sit down with one to pick his brain.

He walked through Christopher Dowd's doorway, the office welcoming him with lounge chairs and a fully stocked kitchen. *This is it,* he thought. *This is where I belong.*

Chris Dowd rose from behind his desk and approached Jeremy with an extended hand.

"Jeremy, nice to meet you. Not many on your level will reach out in this manner. I'm happy to give you some of my time today."

Jeremy's mind raced as he took in his surroundings. Chris had a wall-sized board with all the players' names, from Mike Trout to Bryce Harper.

"Thank you for your time, Mr. Dowd," Jeremy said, focusing on controlling his nerves.

"It's my pleasure. I was once in your shoes, working in ticketing, and eventually worked my way up to where I am today."

"My dream is to work in the front office," Jeremy said. "I would love to hear your story."

"Of course. Let's take a seat." Chris led them across the office to where two lounge chairs faced each other. Chris sat down, elbows planted on his knees. Jeremy noticed his hair was freckled salt and pepper and crow's feet nestled beneath his eyes. *Stressful job,* he thought. Chris was only in his mid-forties.

"I started in the ticket office with the Baltimore Orioles, taking calls and selling tickets on game days." Chris's tone soothed Jeremy's nerves. "I focused on being the best at what I did. If I could sell the most tickets, then I could be promoted."

"How did you go about it?" Jeremy asked.

"I believe in two things, Jeremy: Be so good they can't ignore you. That's step one. And, two, I believe God put us all on this planet to help each other. If you're serious about having a career in this industry, just keep your head down and work as hard as you can. Be the best."

"I can do that," Jeremy replied. He hadn't had more than two interviews in his life, so he didn't know what else to ask. "Thank you so much for your time today."

Chris showed him around his office before walking him back to the stairwell.

"Let me know if you need anything at all," Chris said.

"Thank you, Mr. Dowd. I look forward to my future here."

Jeremy strutted back to the call center. *I'm gonna make it. I'm gonna do big things in baseball.*

"Where were you?" Lewis asked when Jeremy returned to his desk.

He leaned in toward Lewis, and whispered, "Chris Dowd's office." Jeremy sat back with a smirk, and watched as Lewis blinked his droopy eyes.

In eleven seasons at the same desk, three different managers, and two directors, Lewis had seen it all. "That's good," Lewis said. "People who get in good with them upstairs usually wind up there themselves."

4

December 2010

Jeremy had never felt the need to drink. Offer him a joint and he'd smoke it without hesitation. But in high school his friends drank before every football game, and they acted like complete assholes. Booze had never interested him.

"Maybe on my twenty-first," he often told his best friend, Ronnie. That day was fast approaching in January, and he would inevitably have his first drink.

But what Jeremy was most excited about had nothing to do with liquor.

Poker.

Over the past two years he'd played in friends' home games and some weekly games run in bars that Lewis helped him get into. "We don't play for money, so it's not considered gambling," one of the bar owners told him early on. "As long as you don't drink, I don't have an issue with you here." Jeremy always respected the rules, grateful for the opportunity.

Even though money wasn't involved, he took the games seriously. He had learned how to read tells and practiced some of the advanced strategies he had read in books written by the pros. In the bars, he learned the most important lesson: *Never play poker drunk.* So many times, a respectable opponent would build up a stack of chips early, only to see them diminish as the night carried on and the whiskey flowed.

As Lewis said, "This is a game of judgment, and if your ability to judge is impaired, you lose. Plain and simple."

From the time Jeremy won his first live tournament, he was hooked. Beating his friends and winning their money was fun, but the look on people's faces when an underage kid came in and beat them out of a free bar tab was the best.

Bar tournaments consisted of three types of players: regulars, beginners, and poker players. The regulars had the biggest motivation to win, as the prize was typically a fifty-dollar credit toward their tab. They understood the basics of the game and could outlast many beginners and some of the poker players. Of the thirty or so players that participated, this group made up half.

The beginners usually just happened to be drinking at the bar and figured they would take a crack at playing. They would ask what hand beat what, and would receive a cheat sheet explaining. They always seemed to take their cards off the table and hold them up to their eyes like an old lady trying to read the newspaper. Jeremy referred to these players as "the bank," since he would gouge them for all their chips right off the bat.

Thank you and drive safe, he would think as the beginners walked away, unsure why they had lost. Every game needed these beginners so everyone else could build up their stacks and get down to business.

The poker players consisted of a handful of players who showed up to sharpen their skills and utilize new strategies, and always ended up at the final table. Jeremy considered himself part of this group; he played to win and learn, and hated the drunks who interrupted the flow of the game with their slow decision-making.

"Don't come in here on your twenty-first and put me out of business with all those gift cards you have piling up," his favorite bar owner had recently said with a smirk.

5

May 2011

"Congrats, man," Ronnie slurred. "You made it!"

Ronnie squeezed Jeremy, the stench of whiskey oozing from his pores. Jeremy returned a half-hearted embrace, not feeling too sober himself. Five months had passed since his twenty-first birthday, and this was probably the most he'd had to drink in all that time. But Ronnie was almost double Jeremy's size, and still he leaned on his best friend to keep from face-planting on their living room floor.

The night of partying had finally come to a close, and Jeremy guessed Ronnie had had an entire bottle of Jack Daniels, along with some celebratory shots of tequila.

Ronnie had been the one to volunteer his and Jeremy's apartment for the after-party—after they closed down the local bar with a group karaoke rendition of "Don't Stop Believin'."

"Come over to our place! Let's keep this party going," Ronnie had slurred.

Only two others had been able to keep up with Ronnie: Jeremy's girlfriend, Jamie, and a friend from high school, Eric. The four of them packed into the Toyota Prius that came to pick them up, Ronnie taking shotgun with pleasure. He loved to talk the ear off of the driver, which always made for an entertaining ride home.

"Good evening, Mohammed," Ronnie greeted their driver. "Or should I say good morning!"

The driver nodded skeptically, probably worried about his car's upholstery.

"I hate to be *that* guy," Ronnie continued. "But would you mind stopping at McDonald's on the way? I could use something in my belly besides booze." He slapped his gut as he said this and let out an awkward chuckle.

"Yes, sir," Mohammed responded, revealing a thick Middle Eastern accent.

"My man, Mohammed," Ronnie said. He ran his hand through his black hair, which was ruffled after the long night of partying. "I know you can't accept tips, but I might forget a ten-spot when I get out, if you know what I mean."

Mohammed nodded, but his polite smile suggested he had no clue what Ronnie meant.

Jeremy closed his eyes in the backseat of the Prius, trying to block out the voices at the drive-thru. His churning stomach distracted him from the pounding of his head. He had reached his limit, and he knew his own after-party would have to consist of water if he wanted a chance of avoiding a ferocious hangover.

Ronnie said an enthusiastic good-bye to Mohammed, tucking a ten under the visor with a clumsy swagger, and they all stumbled toward the front door. The porch light revealed a group of moths flickering around in the warm night.

Jamie, Jeremy's girlfriend, wrapped an arm around his waist to help him from stumbling, though she'd had plenty to drink as well. Her warm body against his, the fruity smell radiating from her dark brown hair... Ronnie once told him that sex prevented hangovers—why not find out? She lived half an hour away, but had brought her overnight bag, which usually had lingerie inside. They'd only been together two months, and they couldn't keep their hands off each other.

Ronnie jiggled his key into the lock as he swatted at the moths flapping around his head. He flipped on the light switch to reveal the streamers hanging from the ceiling in the living room and the bottles of alcohol covering the dining room table.

The apartment had been immaculate at the beginning of the night. All through high school, Ronnie had kept himself and his car in a respectable state, so it wasn't until they moved in together during college that Jeremy learned his best friend was a closet slob.

"Welcome to the after party, folks!" Ronnie exclaimed, plopping down on the couch to finish his burger and fries. Ronnie powered on the TV, chose the "'90s hits" channel, and MC Hammer danced across the screen in his parachute pants.

Jamie stepped away to use the bathroom inside Jeremy's master bedroom. Eric joined Ronnie on the couch and cracked open two cans of beer with a drunken grin.

Ronnie rose from the couch with his beer and wobbled over to Jeremy. He reminded Jeremy of the stereotypical mummy, hands raised in front of his body and a side-to-side stride.

Ronnie wrapped a flabby arm around him. "You're gonna do big things. Hotshot doctor. Doctor Heston here to mind-fuck you."

Jeremy had graduated with a bachelor's degree in psychology, but planned to pursue a master's and help others fight depression. Ronnie had graduated the week prior with a degree in business and looked forward to helping Jeremy open his future practice.

"Yeah, right," Jeremy said. "I'll have real clients to help. You two dipshits are the only ones I'll mind-fuck!"

Ronnie slapped him on the back and returned to the couch.

Jeremy pulled his cell phone out and groaned at the 2:35 flashing on the screen. A text message had come in a couple minutes before, from Jamie.

He opened the text and, to his delight, a picture of his naked girlfriend filled up the screen. The photo was mostly dark, with the exception of her face. She looked tired in the eyes but her warm smile seduced him. He could tell she was lying in bed from the way her hair splayed out behind her head, covering most of the pillow beneath her.

The real party is in here, the text read.

Jeremy felt the blood rushing to his crotch.

"Think I'm gonna call it a night," Jeremy said. Eric was passed out on the arm of the couch, a pool of drool forming on the fake leather.

"Word, bro," Ronnie replied sleepily. "See you in the morning."

"Thanks again for tonight, Ron. Good night."

In his bedroom, Jeremy found Jamie naked under the sheets. He slid into bed with her and her body warmed him up.

Life is good, he thought as Jamie climbed on top of him.
*****

The sunlight clawed its way through the closed blinds. Jeremy felt like a stake had been driven into his brain. When they were first dating he had joked to Jamie about being a cheap date: two drinks was all it took for him to feel a solid buzz, while a third guaranteed drunkenness.

Ten, he thought back to the prior night. *Ten fucking drinks.* Regardless, he could clearly recount everything that had happened. From the first shot of tequila to Jamie riding him like a mechanical bull. Twice—though it hadn't prevented a hangover as Ronnie had promised. Jeremy cursed him internally. Even the muted daylight shot pain into his mind.

The bed sheets had been kicked off, and Jeremy lay naked on the mattress, alone. Jamie was gone, but her duffel bag still rested in the corner of his room.

The clock on his nightstand seemed to judge him. Almost noon.

A whirlpool of alcohol spun in his belly, and his lips were so dry they hurt his tongue when he licked them.

The sound of muffled music came through his closed door. He planted his feet on the carpet and stumbled across piles of clothes and sheets to his bathroom. He pulled his black robe from the door and slung it over himself as he headed for the living room.

The TV shared facts about Justin Timberlake as he sang and danced in the background. *Way to go, guys. Left the damn TV on all night.* He was too hungover to give a shit. Eric was in the same position, hunched over the arm of the couch. He snored quietly, an idle engine compared to the roaring V8 sound coming from Ronnie's bedroom.

Drunken nights with Ronnie always included two things: a trip to McDonald's, and a booming snore loud enough to wake Dracula from his coffin. *Some things will never change.*

Jeremy noticed his keys were missing from the key rack beside the front door, which meant Jamie had gone out. *Please bring me something, anything to help this* fucking *headache.*

He could smell alcohol each time he exhaled, pushing his gag reflex to its limit. He shuffled into the kitchen, and filled a glass with water from the sink.

Eric stirred, then sat up straight, black hair frazzled in every direction, a streak of dried drool white against his brown skin.

"What the *fuck* happened last night?" he asked in a groggy voice, after turning to see Jeremy standing in the kitchen.

"Well, we went to Shady's, met some friends, got fucked up, and came here. You and Ronnie kept drinking and you passed out right there, with the TV on all night."

Eric gave him a blank stare with bloodshot eyes. He pulled his phone from the couch cushions, only to toss it aside when he discovered its dead battery. Mustering his energy, he shouted, "Ron, get your sorry ass out here!"

A sound somewhere between a cough and a dry heave responded from behind the closed door.

"Ron had one of his nights," Eric said. "Remember the ride home?"

"Poor Mohammed." Jeremy shook his head.

"Mohammed loved me, dickhead!" Ronnie appeared in his doorway, wearing a too-tight wife-beater and baggy pair of boxers. He crossed his arms as he fought off hiccups. "Sorry you bitches couldn't hang last night."

Eric had fallen back to sleep, his body across the whole couch now.

Jeremy heard a car door slam outside, and Ronnie craned his neck to see out the window.

"Damn, bro, you sent her out for breakfast?" Jamie opened the door holding a familiar pink box, from their favorite doughnut place. "Guess she's not too bad."

"Shut up, dude," Jeremy whispered under his breath.

Ronnie and Jamie had clashed on many things, not the least of which was relationships. Their heated discussions had often left Jeremy feeling stuck in the middle.

Ronnie insisted happiness came only from one's self, not someone else. After a string of failed relationships, Ronnie swore to not enter another relationship until he was thirty, claiming that all girls in their twenties were crazy bitches.

"They're fun in the sack, but once they try for more, it's game over," Ronnie had explained to Jeremy.

Jamie, on the other hand, may as well have lived a life from a cheesy romantic comedy. She thought she'd found true love with Jeremy, even though they had practically just started dating.

They'd met in a creative writing class during their first semester at Denver State University. They were both involved with someone else, but maintained a low-key friendship over the next four years.

And then, on the first day of the spring semester of their senior year, early in the morning, Jeremy was passing through the courtyard behind the library when he noticed Jamie sitting on a bench with her face buried in her hands. For January in Denver, the weather was surprisingly warm. Jeremy crossed the grass, which was still covered with morning dew.

"Jamie?" he asked as he approached. Her dark hair glowed in the sunlight. He noticed her shoulders shaking, and though she kept her face between the palms of her hands, he could hear her muffled sniffles as he approached.

Jamie raised her head, revealing streams of tears down her cheeks. "CJ broke up with me last night," she managed to say in a composed voice. "He said he doesn't want to be in a long-distance relationship during college." Her lips quivered.

"It's fucking senior year, and now it's a problem?"

"I'm sorry, Jamie." Jeremy debated embracing her. "I don't know what to say."

"It's fine," she said, wiping at her face and drawing in a deep inhale. "I'm just glad you're here."

Jeremy said, "Bad things always lead to good things, don't forget."

Jamie nodded in agreement, even as a new batch of tears rolled down her smooth, soft face.

"How about we skip class and go grab breakfast. I know a great spot." Jeremy softened his tone.

"But it's the first d—"

"Exactly. All we do on the first day is read the syllabus. C'mon, let's go."

He took a step back and waited to see if she would follow. He was surprised to see Jamie gather her stuff and join him.

"So where are we going?" she asked.

"It's called The Hen's Den. They have the best—"

"Pancakes!" Jamie finished. "Fuck, yes, let's go. I'm gonna eat a whole big stack of the Reese's pancakes!"

I love a girl who can cuss, Jeremy thought as they crossed the courtyard.

*****

Jeremy and Ronnie sat on their deck. Their hangovers were finally gone, along with their guests. Above them, on the awning over their heads, the rain fell so hard it sounded like applause.

They sat across from each other at a round table where they spent many summer nights, having a conversation they'd had many times before.

"I don't get why you wanna go down this road," Ronnie said,

sipping a bottle of beer. "We're young. We have so much freedom. No more school. Just work and partying. But you wanna throw it away to be tied down and play house?"

Jeremy paused, then said carefully, "Look. I know we'll never see eye to eye on this. All I can do is follow my heart."

Ronnie stared at his bottle, avoiding eye contact. "You're gonna do what you're gonna do," he said in a flat tone, staring out at the rain. "But I can't support you. I know that's a fucked-up thing to say, but it's how I feel."

Jeremy sat in silence, feeling like Ronnie had punched him in the gut. He rationalized that Ronnie was just tense from Jamie having been around all day. "To each his own," he managed. *You're pathetic.*

"Our lease ends in four months," Ronnie said roughly. "Maybe you should just move in with her then."

Jeremy's background in psychology meant he knew better than to fall for Ronnie's nonsensical trap. Arguing with him reminded Jeremy of arguing with a teenager: cheap insults and mind games.

"Bro, you just need to chill," Jeremy tried.

"Don't even start with your psycho-babble bullshit!" Ronnie snapped. "You've already changed since you started seeing her. I used to never be able to shut you up about changing the world or revolutionizing psychology. Now it's nothing but your cocksucking puppy love!"

Jeremy couldn't deny it: his focus *had* shifted to Jamie lately. Interest in his job had faded, and now his friendship with Ronnie had suffered. Their weekly dinner and drinks had stopped as his relationship developed.

"You know what, this is good," Ronnie said. "I think it's time to go our separate ways. We don't agree on anything these days."

You little bitch, Jeremy thought. "So are we breaking up?" he asked mockingly.

Ronnie didn't even crack a smile as he continued to gaze out at the rain. "I just don't think we need to live together anymore."

No shit, Jeremy thought. *I'm going to change the world, and you're going to stay here and get drunk in your underwear.*

"Okay, Ron. So be it."

6

J une 2011

Weeks passed and the argument became a distant memory. It wasn't the first time they disputed love and life, and it wouldn't be the last.

Ronnie, however, continued to insist on the termination of their living arrangement, and the idea had grown on Jeremy.

They had made memories that would last a lifetime in their three years living together: nights getting drunk and high to philosophize life and hot tubbing in their community pool.

Jeremy wouldn't trade those memories for the world, but he always considered the future. Ronnie lived in the moment, but Jeremy wanted to prepare for what came next.

His relationship had progressed with Jamie since the argument in the rain, which had caused more tension between her and Ronnie. Fortunately, they worked opposite shifts, so their encounters at the apartment were rare.

Jeremy envisioned Jamie in his future. He thought—he actually thought—maybe they could find a place together and truly share a life.

Graduation had changed everything. Aside from now having a BS in psychology, he also had plenty of free time. He had always taken a course or two during summers and hadn't had real time off for years.

With no responsibilities after the work day ended, he enjoyed going to the bars downtown to spend his poker money. Jamie worked the closing shift at a pizzeria near the stadium. Summertime, no homework, and drinking with friends. Life couldn't get any better.

And then it did.

Sammy informed him of an open position: assistant for the outbound sales team. "You've worked so hard," he said, "we want to offer you this position before anyone else."

Jeremy felt adrenaline pump through him. He was even close with Marisa, who had never mentioned searching for other jobs.

"I accept," Jeremy said, unable to keep the grin off his face. "What great timing." Positions rarely opened up during the season, and certainly not so soon after Opening Day.

"Beautiful. Glad to hear it. You're joining one of the best teams in the organization and will play a vital role in their success."

"When do I start?" Jeremy asked.

*****

After work, Jeremy decided to go out for dinner to celebrate. He walked to the popular pizzeria where Jamie worked. The neon sign on the building's facade welcomed him to Deep Dish. He passed through the clouds of smoke on the patio and opened the door to the rich smell of Chicago-style pizza. A young girl greeted him from the hostess stand.

He asked for a table in Jamie's section and she guided him through the bar into the main dining room. The restaurant was quiet, as the after-work crowd hadn't filled in yet. The hostess led him to a table overlooking the street.

Jamie approached the table and put a hand on Jeremy's

shoulder. She couldn't kiss or hug him while on the clock. "Hey! How was your day?"

"I got a promotion."

"A promotion?" Jamie asked, her jaw dropping. Jeremy loved how cute she looked in her work uniform with her hair pulled back into a ponytail, revealing big hazel eyes and high cheek bones. "You didn't tell me you applied for a promotion."

"I didn't." Jeremy turned from the window to face her. "They picked me for this job opening and offered it on the spot. I start tomorrow."

"Wow, babe, how exciting. I should be off around eight if you want me to come and celebrate with you."

"That sounds nice. You should stay the night."

"Maybe. We'll see how the night goes." They hadn't had much alone time in the previous month due to their conflicting schedules. Jeremy feared they might be drifting apart. In the beginning they'd spent every night together, regardless of their schedules.

"I really want to see you. I'll even wait here till you get off." Jeremy wanted to discuss his concerns with Jamie.

She gave a shy grin as she blushed, something she hadn't done in a while. "Well, I guess if I must...." She kept a tight-lipped smile. "Let me go get you a burger."

Jeremy waited in the booth and pondered how to approach the conversation later that night. Jamie wasn't one for confrontation—he'd even seen her throw fits of rage if a discussion didn't go the way she liked. But still, he figured getting his feelings out in the open would be much healthier than bottling it all in.

Jamie returned with a burger and a tall lemonade. "I'm off at eight. Just confirmed with my boss. Don't worry about staying, I'll be over around 8:30." She put a hand on his shoulder, and Jeremy remembered how much he loved her despite their issues.

"Oh, good. We can watch some stand-up and relax. Haven't done that in a while."

"That's not all we haven't done in a while." She grinned, knowing she could seduce her boyfriend as easily as tying her shoes. As Jamie walked away, his leg bounced up and down like Thumper from *Bambi.*

He attacked his burger with vigor while Jamie tended to a couple other tables. For a pizzeria, Jeremy thought they served perfect burgers.

*****

Jeremy arrived home just as the sun set behind the Rocky Mountains, filling the sky with a strong, orange glow. Ronnie was at work and wouldn't get in until midnight.

On his drive home, Jeremy had decided his serious talk with Jamie would have to wait. He was on top of the world and he didn't want anything to bring him down. Instead he wanted to use the evening to try and rekindle their flame in a more natural way.

He went straight for the kitchen when he walked in and poured a rum and Coke. The clock on the microwave read 7:55, glowing green. He slammed his drink and poured another. Two drinks in, he always felt his inner confidence soar through the roof.

He sat down to watch some Louis C.K., and before he knew it there was a knock at the door. He pulled it open to find Jamie leaning against the door frame.

"Hey!" he said, moving aside to let her in. "Do you want a

drink?"

"No thanks," she said, putting her purse on the love seat next to the couch. "Are you drunk, babe?" Jamie asked, noticing the half empty glass on the floor and the bottle of rum on the kitchen counter.

"Nah, it's only my first glass." Some lies had to be told to avoid judgment.

"You know what, go ahead and pour me one. We have to celebrate." Jamie walked into the bathroom.

Jeremy made her one and then topped off his own glass. He grabbed both glasses and went to find her.

She stood in the bathroom doorway, naked from head to toe, her hair hanging down to her breasts. Jeremy froze in his tracks.

"Why don't you put those cups down and come join me?"
*****

They lay in the dark room, listening to the sounds of their breath slowing.

"Are we okay?" Jamie asked suddenly.

"You tell me," Jeremy said, surprised.

"I don't know. It seems like we've been more busy than ever since school finished."

"We just need to make more of an effort to see each other."

Silence fell, leaving only the rumblings of the TV in the next room.

Jeremy felt Jamie sit up beside him, and even in the pitch-black room he could feel her staring at him.

"I'm going," she said, her voice devoid of emotion. The sheets ruffled as she pushed them down, and the coolness of the night covered Jeremy's bare body.

Here we go again, he thought. "Why are you leaving?" he

asked, bracing for another one of her tantrums.

"You think *we* need to make more of an effort?" Jamie snapped. "*I* make plenty of effort. *You* get drunk. Seems like you can't go a day without drinking."

I only drink to deal with you. Of course he didn't dare say this out loud.

"Babe, just get back in bed and take a deep breath," Jeremy said. "We can talk about this."

"Nope. Good night." She stormed out of the bedroom, the glow of the TV flashing in. Jeremy heard the front door open and slam shut.

Headlights blared through his window, making him squint, and he jumped out of bed to look through the blinds just in time to see the headlights pull back and drive away.

She's out of her fucking mind. Jeremy's stomach dropped. He hated confrontation.

He grabbed his cell phone to call her. Her voicemail picked up after one ring.

"What did I do?" he whispered to his empty room.

7

October 2011

The remainder of baseball season zipped by, leaving the Bears behind as the postseason started. Jeremy had enjoyed working with the outbound sales team. The move from the call center provided more face time with the club's executives, and he greeted them every time they walked by. His new manager, Matthew Harris, was a bit of a tight-ass, but seemed to relax as long as all the work got completed.

Jeremy sat down in Matt's office one afternoon and looked out the window at downtown Denver. A small flood of people squeezed by one another on the sidewalks during the lunch rush.

Matt typed on his laptop from across his polished desk. His office was clutter-free, nothing on his desk but a pen and notepad. A matching cherry wood shelving unit stood against the wall behind Matt, and was also free of anything but a framed picture of his wife, smiling a cheesy grin with her platinum-blond hair flowing behind her as she leaned back in an awkward pose.

Matt had never spoke of his wife or delved into his personal life at all in the five months working with Jeremy.

"What are you working on today?" Matt asked, looking up

from the screen with his beady black eyes.

"I'm finishing up the season reports." Jeremy slouched back in his seat, trying to relax.

"I wanted to fill you in on the game plan moving forward," Matt said. His black fauxhawk seemed extra stiff today. "At the end of this week, you'll be going back into the call center for the remainder of the off-season."

Jeremy stared at him blankly. "And I'll come back once we get close to the season?" Jeremy did his best to hide the panic in his voice.

Matt looked down at his crossed hands on his desk. "We'll be evaluating the position as a whole come springtime, and will let you know at that point." Matt gave Jeremy a blank stare. "Thank you for all your help this season."

Did I just get demoted back to the fucking call center? A tick of anger arose in him, and shock spread its way through his body.

"Okay. Thanks." He stood up and returned to his desk across the hall, staring blindly at his computer screen and trying to figure out what just happened.

Was it the fucking Pray at the Park Day? Jeremy wondered, thinking back. Matt had offered Jeremy the chance to meet the Christian rock band performing for the event, but Jeremy had no interest and ended up not going despite being at the game.

Pray at the Park Day was a special event created by Matt a few years back. August always was low in ticket sales, so he reached out to Christian churches in the area and got a local Christian rock band to play a post-game concert.

The event showed instant results, selling 30,000 tickets for a game that normally averaged 20,000. Matt ran with the success the following season and started promoting the event before the season started. He had managed to persuade the owners to hire the hottest Christian band in the country, The Revelations.

Word spread about the concert and tickets for Pray at the Park sold out by June, two months ahead of the date. Matt pulled in nearly a million dollars from the event, and earned his promotion to the director of outbound sales.

In 2010, Jeremy attended the event for his first and last time. He sat in his usual left-field bleacher seats. The dry heat beat down on the crowd on day games in July and August. The stadium's 50,000 seats all being full caused an extra level of discomfort as people in the bleachers squished together.

Wrong day to not have my own seat, he thought as a wheezing woman sat next to him with her two young boys. The woman had her dark red hair in a ponytail over her sun visor. The bill of the visor had small crucifixes pinned to each side. She wore a purple shirt with an image of angel wings spread apart around a baseball that read "St. Matthew's" across the middle.

Oh, God, Jeremy thought, realizing he was in the middle of a large church group fresh out of Sunday morning mass. The two boys yapped to their mother, begging for hot dogs. They had the same purple shirts, and streaks of sunscreen across their arms and face.

"If you sit still and relax, we'll get hot dogs after the game starts."

The boys, obviously brothers, dropped their heads and sat back on the bleachers with their arms crossed.

"Don't ever have boys if you can help it," she leaned over and whispered to Jeremy. He returned a kind chuckle, keeping his eyes fixed on the grounds crew putting their final touches on the field.

More purple shirts crowded the section, along with small crucifixes, Bibles, and a handful of *John 3:16* signs.

"Praise God for such a beautiful day!" a man shouted from the front row, getting a collective "Amen!" from those surrounding him.

What the fuck? Jeremy suddenly felt anxious. He was a Catholic, but too much was too much.

His parents had raised him to never judge or discount other religions, but the park was packed with hard-core Christians—and they weren't afraid to force their agenda onto others. Pray at the Park was supposedly open to all faiths, but a quick look around suggested otherwise.

A church choir proceeded to sing the National Anthem and the crowd hummed along. Beads of sweat dripped down Jeremy's back.

"Please remain standing for a word from our very own Steph Johnson," the PA announcer said.

The crowd roared as the team's left fielder strolled to the microphone behind home plate.

"Welcome everyone to Pray at the Park, what a great turnout!" Steph said to more applause. "I wanted to take a moment to lead us in a pre-game prayer. In the name of the Father, the Son, and the Holy Spirit."

At least 90 percent of the crowd bowed their heads in unison.

"Heavenly Father, we gather here today as one, to honor you on this beautiful Sabbath. Please keep all of us safe today. We on the team thank You for this tremendous opportunity to play professional baseball. We look forward to an afternoon of fun in Your name. Amen."

Forty thousand people thundered a strong "Amen" together and ruptured back into applause as Steph Johnson trotted back to the dugout. Jeremy's phone buzzed in his pocket. It was Jamie.

"Hello there."

"Hey babe, how's it going? I have a few minutes on my break, just wanted to check in."

"Well, this is gonna be an interesting game." He lowered his voice and cupped a hand over his mouth. "There's a bunch of Jesus freaks here."

"I'm sure you'll be fine," she chuckled.

"I might have to get out of here."

"Sorry, babe. I'll call you when I get off."

What happened to keeping religion separate from other things? There's no need to be praying at a baseball game.

He rose from his seat, stepping into the aisle. His employee badge granted him access to the underground tunnels to surpass the herd of people surely gathered on the concourse. He took the stairs to the bottom of the section and gave a nod to the section's regular beer vendor, an old, crazy-looking man with a handlebar mustache and peanut earrings.

At the bottom his favorite usher, Barb, greeted him. Her short and scrawny frame combined with her snow-white hair made her seem nonthreatening, but she could pounce on rowdy fans like an attack dog.

"Hey, young man. How are you doing today?" she asked with a grin. Her teeth glowed against her sun-soaked skin, which had absorbed plenty of rays over the years.

"Barb, great to see you. Gonna head up to the office for a bit to cool down."

"Of course. I'll see you around." She patted his back as he

walked by her toward the tunnel.

He swung open the large steel door and the smells of hot dogs, popcorn, and beer gave way to the musty stench of the underground. The sounds of the crowd and the announcer became muffled.

The tunnel had its own behind-the-scenes world of activity. Concession workers ran around in chaos, while ushers socialized during their breaks. Security led a stumbling man to the underground holding cell, clearly one of the few in the crowd who skipped morning mass.

Jeremy nodded to the security guard as he passed. The usual staff stood guard outside of the teams' locker rooms and gave friendly grins to Jeremy as he walked by. He reached the elevator behind home plate and took it to the first floor, where staff were sparse during games.

In the call center, he was surprised to see Herman Jeffries at a desk in the back row. Herman only worked about six hours each month and still had access to two tickets for all eighty-one games of the season. Lewis had warned Jeremy about him, claiming he was bad company and an all-around cheapskate.

Herman sat directly in front of Sammy's office, reclined with his hands behind his head, and a tight polo shirt showing bulging muscles. His blonde hair appeared freshly buzzed, and he looked at Jeremy from behind the glasses that rested on his pointy nose.

"Hey there, cowboy," Herman said. Jeremy had noticed that he never called anyone by their actual name.

"Hey, Herman. What you up to?"

"Just watching the game from here." He nodded to the tube TV at the front of the room. The Bears had just surrendered a home run. "I like to watch the game muted. Our commentators are total shit."

"Very true," Jeremy agreed with a grin.

"Besides, all those Bible thumpers are out there. I'm A-okay in here."

Jeremy nodded, noticing that Herman had his computer on and the ticketing software open. "What you doing there?"

"Oh, just some research for my other job," Herman said, narrowing his eyes as he assessed Jeremy. "How would you like to make some extra money on the side?" His eyes reminded Jeremy of a snake.

"What do you mean?"

"Have you ever heard of the term *opportunity cost*?" Herman asked.

Jeremy looked around the call center to confirm no one was within earshot, then shook his head.

"I learned about it in my economics class," Herman said. "It's the idea that items are worth exactly what someone is willing to pay for them.

"For example, say you have a ticket for the Super Bowl that has a face value of a hundred dollars. Now say I come and offer you a thousand dollars for that same ticket and you reject my offer. Even though you only paid one hundred, the ticket actually *cost* you a thousand because I was willing to give you that amount. You had the *opportunity* to make a grand. Make sense?"

"Yeah. Sort of," Jeremy replied, lowering his brow.

"It makes more sense when you see it in action. I apply this theory to event tickets and resale them to the black market, where opportunity costs run wild."

"So you're a scalper?"

"Of course not. You won't see me in the street trying to hustle people. This is pure business, a microeconomics principle."

"So you're doing this with Bears tickets?" Jeremy asked, becoming more intrigued.

"I do it for all big events in town. Concerts, sports, whatever is going on. It all depends on the buzz of the event. For the Bears, it's really just Opening Day, fireworks games, and when they play someone like the Yankees or Red Sox."

Jeremy nodded. Herman had never said more than five words to him, and now he couldn't stop talking.

"Anyway," Herman said. "I don't wanna talk about this too much here. But think it over and let me know, cowboy." He gave Jeremy an awkward wink and returned his attention to the game.

"Good talking to you, Herman. I'll see you around." Jeremy left the call center, trying to wrap his head around the exchange. *No way Herman can be trusted. He doesn't even know me and tried to recruit me into his scheme.*

Jeremy had had enough for the day and left the stadium. He drove home in silence, thinking over what Herman had said. Nine dollars an hour was hard to live off of, but his dream of becoming the team's psychologist weighed too important. He knew he'd need to keep working hard and stay clean in order to get where he wanted to go.

*****

Jeremy never saw Herman again. Rumor had it that he came into some money and no longer needed to waste eight hours a month for free tickets. Jeremy knew the truth, and couldn't help daydreaming about making such easy money.

His screen turned black; he'd just been sitting staring at it and hadn't touched it in twenty minutes. *What does it matter? I'm going back to the dungeon next week.* He felt sick to his stomach. *Why should I be punished for not wanting to meet some Christian band I've never heard of? I don't listen to this shit.*

The salesmen gathered across the hallway at Dillon's desk. Dillon Shaw had brought in more than one million dollars for the team over the course of the season. Jeremy had generated the sales reports at the end of each week, so he always knew who was performing well.

Dillon faced Jeremy's desk, but was blocked by a couple guys hovering in front of Dillon's computer. They whispered, and he could only assume they were gossiping about him.

Disappointment wrapped its claws around Jeremy's gut, and the mix of rage and sorrow made him feel lightheaded and nauseous. *I fucking made it out of the call center. Now I'll be lucky to ever see the light of day again.*

His desk was right outside the call center, so he always saw his friends pass by. Lewis came around the corner at his usual slow pace.

"Hey, Jeremy, how's it going?" Lewis asked.

"Okay. I'm gonna call you after work."

"Sounds good," Lewis replied nonchalantly, and continued to the call center.

Jeremy spent the afternoon looking at job postings online. He supposed he could be overreacting, but his instinct told him otherwise. Matt seemed to be hiding something.

Jeremy remembered what Herman had taught him about opportunity cost, and decided the time had come to take a deeper look.

8

*J*anuary 2012

"So you can't do anything at all for me?" Jeremy asked, fighting the urge to yell. Sammy avoided eye contact as he shriveled behind his desk.

"Look, Jeremy. I wish I could, but I have no say in the matter."

"You're the *manager.* How can you have no say?" Jeremy shot an aggressive look across the desk.

"It doesn't work like that, and you know it. Money decisions always come from the top. This is professional sports." Sammy pursed his lips and sat back in his chair.

Jeremy had just had his annual review, as was the case every January. Four years had passed and he still hadn't received a raise from nine dollars an hour. No one had: there was supposedly a spending freeze.

"Okay then. Thanks for the talk," Jeremy said as he stood and walked out of Sammy's office.

He sat down at his desk, left his work phone on "Not Ready" status to ignore incoming calls, and played games on his cell phone until lunchtime came forty-five minutes later.

Since his return to the call center in October, everything had seemed to snowball out of control. He went back with an open mind and was still hoping to return to outbound sales until

December came and he was informed that he would not return to the position. Worse, one of the girls that had recently been hired in the call center was chosen to fill the role. Kylie had no prior ticketing experience, nowhere near the knowledge of the Bears that Jeremy had, but she was pretty, tall, and blond. *Bold move for a tight-ass Christian like Matt.*

Sammy launched a team lead program as a growth opportunity within the call center. The team lead would be Sammy's right-hand person and would serve as a primary resource for the rest of the staff. Jeremy didn't want to assume anything, but with four seasons of experience he figured he'd be a lock for the role.

He wasn't. Sammy chose Adam Reichs instead. Adam was a good guy: fresh out of college and with a passion for baseball. But Adam had only spent one season with the team, and still regularly had to ask Jeremy questions about how to do his job.

Jeremy decided his future with the Bears was over. His job hunt expanded as he looked at a wide range of companies.

He came across a start-up company called E-Nonymous, Inc. They operated a call center that received calls from people in need of support with issues like tobacco and gambling addictions. The company's mission was based on helping others, and they exhibited a caring attitude toward their employees: four weeks of paid time off, full health coverage, and nearly triple the pay. Jeremy wasted no time filling out his application, feeling excited for the first time in ages.

I'm getting out of this fucking place and never looking back.

After slogging through the work day, Jeremy returned to his old habit of drinking once he arrived home. His life felt stuck at a standstill. He had moved into his own apartment downtown after parting ways with Ronnie in September—and months later Ronnie still hadn't reached out to him. It was inevitable, but it still bothered him.

With money tight, he focused more free time on sports betting and poker, playing at a friend's house every Sunday night. Most weeks he could guarantee an extra fifty dollars in his pocket, sometimes up to two hundred. He rarely left a loser.

The only issue with the games was the late start time of 9 p.m., sometimes even 10, depending when everyone showed up. This led to late nights, followed by a Monday of dragging his ass to work. His performance suffered as the groggy Monday set him back for the whole week.

It's not like I'm working toward anything anymore.

February brought a lucrative two weeks, as he made more than two thousand dollars thanks to a hot streak of basketball betting. The winnings covered nearly three months of rent, which he stashed aside for that purpose only. All paychecks for the following three months would go to fun: nights out, drinking, and, of course, gambling. He thought he might reinvest some of his winnings.

The Bears' on-sale date for tickets always fell on the second Saturday of February, and he planned on purchasing some Opening Day tickets to test out the opportunity cost theory. Opening Day was a guaranteed sell-out every year, so there would be no better chance to give it a shot.

He needed to keep his side project secret. Not even Jamie could know. She didn't mind the gambling, especially with all the winnings, but she would likely object to a job-jeopardizing decision like this.

Too bad my time here is practically up.

9

ebruary 2012

When the second Saturday of February arrived, Jeremy jumped out of bed with more excitement than usual. He still loved the game of baseball, and the on-sale day marked six weeks until the start of the season.

Jeremy felt the energy as soon as he walked into the call center. On-sale day was the only day of the year that all employees worked together, as everyone was required to answer the phones. He saw faces he hadn't seen since July as thirty people crammed into the office, gorging themselves with the doughnuts Sammy had brought in.

Sammy stood on the elevated step of his office, calling for everyone's attention.

"Thank you all for being here this morning," he spoke in a barely raised voice. "Excuse me!"

The murmurs of chatter gave way to silence and all eyes turned to Sammy.

"Welcome to on-sale day," he continued, no longer needing to shout. "Whether you've been through this before or not, just know it is the most chaotic day of the year. You'll also find it will fly by.

"When the phones come on at ten, expect to see the call queue at over seventy for the first two hours. The majority of these calls will be asking for Opening Day tickets. We have a limited amount available today that will be gone within the first half hour. Do your best to try and upsell these customers to different dates once those are sold out.

"Adam and I will be floating around if you need assistance. I've posted today's seating chart on the board, so be sure to check your spot for the day. We have twenty minutes until the phones come on, so grab some breakfast and get settled in. Any questions?"

Eyes bounced around the silent room.

"Thanks, Sammy," Lewis said lazily.

"Alright, let's get at it," Sammy finished with a clap of his hands.

Conversations resumed as everyone worked their way to the bulletin board. Jeremy wrapped up his small talk with Lewis and checked the seating chart.

Of course I'm upstairs, he thought. *Can't even sit at my own fucking desk for this God-awful day.*

Jeremy stormed out of the call center, ignoring others as he passed.

They used an upstairs office on the suite level on the rare occasions when staff wouldn't fit in the main office. The upstairs office was more depressing than the main one. It was as cold as the city morgue, dust covered the computers, and mice droppings littered the carpet. Jeremy imagined it must be like the working conditions in prison.

He headed for the elevator with his backpack slung over one shoulder. *I'm done. I can't do this shit anymore.* He thought about getting drunk after work before starting on some homework he had to complete, and the thought soothed his mood.

The elevator took him to the suite level, revealing a dim hallway.

"Jesus," he said, stepping out and feeling the instant draft of coldness. He dragged his feet to the door and swiped his badge to enter.

He was the first to arrive, though someone had come up earlier to turn on all the computers. They hummed in unison with the chorus of buzzing fluorescent lights.

He plopped into his assigned seat and opened up the ticketing software. A seating chart had been placed on each desk to show the pricing structure for all games.

Four dollars? he thought, looking at the cheapest available tickets for Opening Day. *Surely someone would pay at least thirty for those.*

Jeremy clicked four tickets and kept them on hold, switching screens as he heard footsteps approach the door. Five of his coworkers strolled in, Adam among them.

"Hey, Jeremy. How's it going, man?" Adam asked as the other four headed to their desks, coffee and doughnuts in hand.

"Good, man. Just getting ready for the morning," Jeremy said.

"Right on. Did you get enough to eat?"

"I did, thanks. I'm gonna run to the bathroom real quick before the phones come on." Jeremy grinned and walked out, needing a second to get his mind together.

He walked to the furthest end of the suite level, pulled out his cell phone, debated calling Jamie, and decided not to since she'd had a late Friday night at work and was likely still asleep.

Thirty back on four. That's almost a thousand percent return.

He walked back to the office with more vigor in his step.

Everyone waited by their phones, ready for the calls to start any minute.

I'm gonna try just those four tickets to see how it works. Jeremy pulled out his credit card and wrote the number down on a sticky note to use once the flood gates opened.

Twenty phones rang in unison, and the volume in the room exploded as everyone answered their phones with "Denver Bears, how can I help you?"

Jeremy glanced over his shoulder and saw Adam on the other side of the aisle. He answered his phone but didn't speak, keeping the mute button pressed down on his headset. His fingers typed quickly as he rushed to purchase the four tickets he'd held.

"Hello?" a voice called in his headset. Jeremy's heart raced. *Sorry, guy, but I need a raise.*

"HELLO!" the voice screamed. "Say something, you shit-heads!" Jeremy imagined a middle-aged man wrapped in his robe, sitting at his kitchen table and eating a bowl of cereal while he called for his Bears tickets.

Done. He completed the transaction, processing the order under Jamie's name to have the tickets sent to her address.

"Motherfuck!" the man shouted, and Jeremy disconnected the call.

No coming back from that one.

He kept the phone off the hook, and a chime beeped in his ear to inform him the next caller had connected. He took the call and processed an Opening Day order for an elderly woman wanting to take her son to the big day. The queue flashed on the phone panel, showing eighty calls waiting.

Gonna be a long fucking morning.

He kept his headset on, his head down, and focused on one

call at a time. The bottle of rum stayed in the back of his mind, waiting for him at home.

*****

"Great work today," Sammy said from behind his desk. "You had 140 calls today, way more than anyone else."

"Thank you," Jeremy replied. His voice echoed in quiet waves around the room. Jeremy felt his stomach quivering, nervous as to why Sammy had called him into his office at the end of the day.

Did he catch my order to Jamie? But she's my girlfriend. I haven't technically done anything wrong.

"I wanted to fill you in on something," Sammy continued.

He can't know. Hundreds of orders were processed today. It's impossible.

"The call center has been asked to help usher at our new tequila bar during day games. There will be upselling and processing payments, and you get to spend some time in the sun. I've decided to send you for Opening Day."

"Oh?" Jeremy questioned, blindsided. The angst immediately drained from his gut. "Well, thank you. I look forward to it."

"Of course," Sammy said. "Look, I know you're in a funk. I want to help."

Then why the fuck did you hire Adam for my role?

"The way things ended for you on Matt's team, I don't agree with. That wasn't fair, but I think you can still move forward here."

Bullshit.

"I appreciate that, Sammy. I look forward to the season ahead."

"As do I. Now go get packed up. I'm about to send everyone

home for the day. Great work today!"

Jeremy returned to the desk upstairs, unsure about how he should feel after his conversation with Sammy. Cheesy motivational posters hung on the walls like it was a middle-school classroom. The dust and mouse shit made it feel like an abandoned attic.

This place blows. This is a terrible company to work for, run by the two biggest slobs in baseball.

He thought back to his second season with the team, when the Bears managed to clinch a postseason berth late in September. As had become standard across baseball, the players celebrated in the clubhouse with bottles of champagne. The staff was invited to join the team in showering themselves in bubbles.

Except for the call center.

"Hey, gang. We're gonna need you to stay on the phones. Customers will be calling to ask about playoff tickets," Sammy had explained at the time, clearly uncomfortable that he was on his way down to the clubhouse and leaving his team behind.

All the call center employees felt a drastic shift in emotions: from celebrating the big victory to sitting in silence, after learning that everyone in the building would be celebrating with the team except for them.

"What the fuck?" Michelle Gardner cried. No one said anything. "Guys, what the fuck?"

Michelle was a Southern girl with no qualms about speaking her mind. Her eyes bulged behind her glasses. "This is bullshit!"

The rest of the call center employees, eight of them including Jeremy, sat in silence at their desks while the TV at the front of the room showed Bears players and employees spraying champagne and beer on one another.

"Guys, I'm sorry this is happening," Jeff Hart said. Jeff was another retired employee working for the free tickets. He always kept a calm approach no matter the situation. "Let me take us all out for drinks after work."

"Jeff, you don't have to pick up the slack for these assholes," Michelle said.

Jeff just nodded.

No one left their desk during the final hour of the workday. The offices and halls outside the call center remained deserted and silent, as all staff had crowded into the players' clubhouse.

The phones never rang.

"Not one fucking call," Michelle said at 4:30, the only words spoken in the office between four and five.

When closing time rolled around, Sammy still hadn't returned to turn off the phones, not that it mattered.

"Let's go grab a drink," Jeremy said, speaking up for the first time all afternoon. "We might as well try to have our own celebration. We made it to the playoffs."

"Yay," Michelle said sarcastically.

"I'm game," Jeff said. "How about you guys?"

Everyone nodded in agreement, except Michelle, who shrugged her shoulders and said, "Sure, I guess."

A bond had formed in a group that was screwed over together. Heads hung, shoulders slumped, and talk remained minimal as they crossed the street to the bar.

The evening turned into a drunkfest. Shots were ordered within seconds of walking in, which led to more and more as the evening passed. By the end of the night, they had tried every type of alcohol the bar had to offer.

Jeff kept his word, despite push-back from the group, and

covered the six-hundred-dollar tab once they decided to call it quits.

Jeremy, Michelle, and Jeff were the last ones standing as the rest faded away.

"What happened today was brutally wrong," Jeff said, sipping from his stein of beer. "I've seen a lot of shit in my time, but can't recall a company ever being so shitty to its employees."

"Amen," Michelle said. "I'm so sick of this. Every week it's something else. We can't even enjoy the team's success because all it means is more work for us to do. More work we won't get any appreciation for."

"I'm not even surprised anymore," Jeremy said. "I've been here four years now and it seems to get worse every day."

"Matt did a number on you," Michelle said. "You did so much for that bastard and he kicks you to the curb like a piece of trash. He's a disgrace to Texas."

Michelle had been hired at the same time as Jeremy, and had always looked out for him.

"You need to get out of this place," Jeff said. "Michelle's right. You were treated like shit and I don't see how you can come back from that. Matt is highly respected by Sue Ellen, so what he says goes." Sue Ellen was the team's vice president of ticketing.

Jeremy nodded. "I know it. And I'm on it. Been applying to jobs, and just waiting to hear back."

"Good for you," Michelle slurred. "I'll be praying for you, Jer."

"Thanks, guys. I should get going." Jeremy stumbled from his bar stool and wrapped an arm around Jeff and one around Michelle. "I love you guys. Thanks for tonight." He kissed them each on the cheek.

"You're a good kid," Jeff said, patting Jeremy on the shoulder. "You good to drive?"

"Yeah," Jeremy lied. "I'll be good with some fresh air."

He walked out of the bar, and the boom of the music gave way to silence as he stepped outside. The cool night welcomed his rising temperature. He felt sweat in his armpits and walked with his arms out to try and cool them off.

He arrived to his car at the stadium lot, sat down, and fell asleep with his keys in hand.

*****

On-sale day had passed and Jeremy still hated his job on Monday morning. He'd reached the point where he felt sick to his stomach at the very sight of the stadium, never mind the stress that came when he entered the building.

This better work, he thought back to the tickets he had purchased.

He had started with the Bears as an eighteen-year-old beginning his freshman year of college. Hope had burned deep in his soul when he joined the team—but perhaps that was just teenage naivete. His motivation had faded as he settled into a routine, working long shifts with no sense of direction.

Jeremy logged into his ticketing system and bought eight more Opening Day tickets under a different name and his second credit card number he typically used for online poker.

He smirked.

It's going to be alright.

10

February 2012

Dr. Adrian Siva looked across his cluttered desk at the squirmy Jeremy Heston. His student never spoke up in classroom discussions and preferred to meet in private after class. Jeremy had a bright mind and a better understanding of the Psychology Disorders course material than any student he could remember.

Their relationship had developed into a mentorship. Jeremy had no clue what he *really* wanted to do in life, so Dr. Siva tried to guide him in the right direction. Dr. Siva's first objection was with Jeremy's job with the Bears. When Jeremy had told him he'd been demoted, he'd offered to use his connections to find Jeremy a psychology internship that would even pay more. But Jeremy had been too proud to accept his help and now, a few months later, was still stuck in a negative thought spiral about the situation.

"I think my ex-boss, Matt, is pushing his own agenda. I didn't fit into his picture so he let me go."

"Why do you say that?"

"Because I'm not like him. He's a judgmental, religious bigot behind closed doors. I told him his Pray at the Park Day was exclusive. Religion shouldn't exclude certain groups of people, especially not at a public gathering like a baseball game. Hell, I went to Catholic high school and even we had Jewish and Muslim students. I don't think any group other than Christians was even invited to this event."

"So you think the event comprised a social inequality?"

"I never thought of it that way, but yes, I do."

"Do you have any proof that this is the reason for your dismissal from the position?" Dr. Siva perked up in his seat, eyebrows raised.

Jeremy thought back through all his encounters with Matt. "No proof," he said, disappointed. "Just my analysis of his behavior."

"Still, I encourage you to continue to think about an instance that might hold up in court. Because I believe you have a potential religious discrimination case."

"That's the problem. *I* never felt discriminated against. I felt his *event* was discriminating. And I just know he's the brains behind the whole thing."

"I see. That actually means a bigger case—against the entire organization."

Here we go, Jeremy thought. He didn't have the energy to even consider what a court case might require of him.

"Jeremy," Dr. Siva continued. "Lawsuit aside. Discrimination aside. You're working toward a master's in psychology. What you do after getting it is what will define you."

"Yes, doctor, I know. We've had this talk before."

"We have. But I don't know if you're understanding me. Our profession is based on the abstract. The mind. Few things about people's thought process can be proven with concrete science." Dr. Siva looked across his desk at Jeremy, studying his student from behind his reading glasses. Streaks of white had started to fill his black hair, complementing the heavy crow's feet forming around his eyes. "This leaves us in a position of uncharted territory. It's our duty to revolutionize our always-changing field of study. Do you understand?"

"Yes, I do," Jeremy said, staring at the scattered papers on Dr. Siva's desk.

"Good. I challenge you to consider what you will do with this—how *you* will change the world. Every discovery that's come before us in our field was found by free thinkers like us. It's our responsibility to continue that mission and, quite frankly, you can't do that from a call center."

"I know." Jeremy sighed. "But psychology is an up-and-coming thing in sports. What if it's part of my big discovery?"

"It may very well be," Dr. Siva said. His face was like a stone, his wrinkles frozen in place. "I just don't want to see you waste your time. You're at the bottom of the totem pole in one of the most competitive industries in the world. And your plan is to work up and into a position that doesn't exist?"

Jeremy stayed silent. He felt like a nuclear bomb had been dropped on his dreams. *Isn't he supposed to support me?*

"Look, this is the purpose of our monthly meetings," Dr. Siva said. "My guidance and opinion. Sometimes the truth is hard to hear."

Jeremy nodded.

"All I'm saying, Jeremy, is to think of how you can influence the world. It won't be by answering phone calls for the next five years. One person can affect millions, never forget that."

Jeremy nodded some more. He felt like a human woodpecker.

"Thank you for our meeting today, Dr. Siva. I definitely have a lot to think about."

"That's all I want to hear," Dr. Siva said, cracking a sly grin.

"The ball's in your court. Please let me know if I can help with anything." Dr. Siva rose from his seat and extended his hand to Jeremy, giving it his usual firm shake.

Jeremy returned the handshake with a smile of relief. *I made it through another of these dumb-ass meetings.*

"Have a good night, doctor," Jeremy said, walking out of the office and down the familiar halls of the psychology building.

*****

Jeremy returned to his apartment after his meeting with Dr. Siva, and lay down on his bed, his mind racing with possibilities. Sometimes his thoughts were so scattered and intense, he wondered if he might have one of the mental illnesses he was studying.

I know I can achieve what I want in baseball. One of the main components of sports psychology was getting players to envision themselves succeeding in the highest-pressure situations. *Close your eyes and see yourself hitting the game-winning home run. Feel the bat in the grip of your palms, and feel the vibrations run up your arms as you make that perfect contact.*

Jeremy tried to apply this logic to himself, but he couldn't find the right words, the right images.

"How do I get there?" he whispered, and he was scared of the quiver in his voice. *I no longer have an obvious way out of the call center.*

He felt anger bubble up in him.

"Matt Harris," he said to his empty room. "You mother-fucker."

He can't get away with treating people like this. It's not fair that such an asshole should have such a big influence on my future.

Jeremy fell asleep, tangled in his thoughts.

11

arch 2012

March brought spring training for the baseball world. Jeremy could taste the hot dogs right around the corner.

Three weeks had passed since he'd purchased the eight Opening Day tickets. He'd posted them for sale on a website called TicketStubs, an online resale marketplace for ticketed events. Anyone could post tickets and set their asking price as they pleased. All that was required was the bar code from the ticket stub, and TicketStubs' software would convert the ticket into an electronic file to be sent anywhere in the world.

Jeremy had an account already created from previous ticket purchases, but he created a separate one to use for his operation. He had purchased the original tickets under Jamie's name, but he wanted to keep her off the record for any of the transactions, so he created the new account under the name Heath Miller. Jeremy was obsessed with Heath Ledger's portrayal of the Joker, and decided to honor him by using his first name. Miller was a common enough name that he wouldn't stand out from the crowd.

The only thing that could trace the tickets back to Jeremy was the linking of his bank account to his TicketStubs profile, to receive payments by direct deposit. That information would only belong to TicketStubs, though, and wouldn't be accessible to anyone in the Bears organization.

With the account created, Jeremy posted his tickets for sale. After much research—TicketStubs provided metrics on average pricing: what had sold, and what hadn't—he decided to post the $4 tickets at an aggressive price of $75 dollars.

Worst-case scenario, I drop them to fifty and still make more than ten times the value.

Now he just had to wait, to find out if Herman's opportunity cost theory really worked.

Less than an hour later, he was looking at an email informing him that $300 would be transferred to his bank account within three business days. "Holy shit," he said. Less than a day later, before the money had even arrived in his account, the remaining four tickets also sold. He had spent $32 and turned it into $600 in the matter of three weeks.

"Okay, this is very real," he told himself. He was at work when the second notification came in, and immediately pulled up the Opening Day seating chart to find nothing available.

That's fine. There'll be more. There always is.

The team released handfuls of tickets on a daily basis. They held on to groups of tickets for special types of reservations, and if they learned the tickets wouldn't be used, they were released to the public for purchase. Opening Day tickets would be snatched up quickly, so he'd have to keep checking.

Jeremy turned his attention to two games later in the schedule. The fireworks games on July 3 and 4 always sold out in advance. *Beautiful,* he thought as he saw plenty of tickets available for both dates. The $4 tickets, in a part of the stadium known as the Bear Cave, would sell for even more on these two nights. Bear Cave tickets granted access onto the field for the fireworks show, and that alone drove up the value of the tickets.

Jeremy had tried the field-view a couple times, and after plenty of kids plowing into him and ashes from the fireworks falling into his hair, he vowed to never do it again.

Make money from people who annoy me and destroy a beautiful baseball field? Don't mind if I do.

Jeremy felt giddy at his future prospects. A familiar tingle filled his stomach, similar to when he peeked at his poker hand to find two aces looking back.

Throughout the day, he bought forty tickets in total, for both games in July. He rotated between his credit cards and had all the tickets mailed to Jamie's address.

Bear Cave tickets would easily sell for a hundred each on TicketStubs, he guessed, and if that were true he would make just shy of four thousand dollars off of those games alone.

A third of what I make during the whole year. He drooled at the thought. *More money than poker, doing less work.*

He planned to post the tickets in June. Nobody would buy a ticket for a hundred bucks when it was still available for four; he'd need to wait until the game sold out.

"Hey all," Sammy said as he walked out of his office. "Just a heads-up that we're releasing about fifty tickets for Opening Day later this afternoon. Not sure at what time, so be sure to keep an eye out for them."

"We sure will!" Jeremy told his boss with a grin. Money might not buy happiness, but it certainly made a dent in his depression.

It's show time, he thought as Sammy hibernated back to his office.

He refreshed his maps. The seating map used color coding

to identify availability, and all seats remained red, meaning not a single seat was available. Yellow indicated minimal availability, while green showed plenty to choose from.

In his four years he had never seen any section turn green for Opening Day. He knew he'd need to be quick on the draw once the seats were released. He was competing against all the people on the team's website looking for tickets at that exact moment.

He sat back, daydreaming about what he wanted to do with his new stream of income. *Maybe I can take Jamie on a trip for our anniversary.*

But after checking every few minutes all day long, by the end of the day, the seats were all still red. Jeremy was disappointed, but he tried hard to not give up hope.

Jamie had a rare night off, and they went out for dinner.

"So how's your little side project?" she asked. She hated when the unmarked, white envelopes started arriving in her mailbox, but Jeremy made a compelling case.

"Very good. I'm making more money than I ever have before. I actually wanted to discuss going to Chicago for our anniversary." Jamie loved to travel, and Chicago was high on her wish list. "I have this extra money now."

"No, Jeremy, that's dirty money. I just don't trust it. Something bad is going to come out of all this."

"I have it under control, please don't worry about it. I can even buy your plane ticket with the money. I insist."

She smiled at the thought. "We'd need to plan the trip fast."

"Then we plan it this weekend and make it happen. I'll even see about getting some Cubs and White Sox tickets."

"Let's do it!" She perked up. "Chi-town, here we come!"

They finished dinner, discussing all the things they could do in the Windy City: deep-dish pizza, the Willis Tower, and the Bean. Jamie created a spreadsheet on her phone to organize their thoughts.

"Just promise me you won't get in too deep with those tickets. You're sure it's not illegal?" Jamie asked.

"'Course not. I'm buying tickets legally. I pay full price like anyone else. And TicketStubs is a giant corporation that focuses on reselling tickets. They wouldn't be there if it was illegal."

12

pril 2012

AOpening Day brought its usual energy. Through some mysterious act of God, Opening Day in Denver always brought out the sun for a beautiful day at the ballpark, while the rest of April the city was buried under blankets of snow.

Jeremy found himself thanking a God he had lost touch with since starting college. *Snow on Opening Day would be catastrophic. At least today will be fun in the sun.* Fans had a habit of calling the call center if there was so much as a cloud in the sky, to ensure the game wasn't delayed or postponed.

"Been blessed with perfect Opening Day weather as long as I've been here," Sammy bragged, knocking on his wooden desk.

Downtown Denver turned into a block party for Opening Day. A parade started at the stadium in the morning, while bars filled up with college students ditching class and businessmen playing hooky for the day in a drunken pregame ritual. This was Jeremy's fifth Opening Day working with the team, so he knew what to expect.

It started in the parking lot, when he arrived for the day. The Bears held back 500 Bear Cave tickets to release three hours before game time. While this happened for every game of the year, Opening Day was the only one where fans camped overnight outside the stadium.

Driving through the parking lot he saw thousands of people lined up, kids running around like it was a playground, and some people even playing games of touch football. Jeremy drove through the masses, then weeded through them after parking his car.

"Hey, buddy, any tickets?" some wise-ass asked as Jeremy walked toward the employee entrance. He kept his head down, knowing it was best to avoid conversation with the fans outside.

"How cool it must be to work for the Bears," a drunk man cried.

Jeremy kept his head down and waved to the security guard as he entered the stadium's tunnel. A new group of game-day staff flooded the walkway, running carts of food and merchandise in every direction in their purple shirts and black pants. The energy of the new season radiated from the tunnel, up to the offices. Executives wore their finest suits. Even Sammy looked sharp.

"Good morning, everyone," Sammy called out to the team as Jeremy sat down at his desk. "Happy Opening Day! My favorite holiday of the year. There will be about 200 seats opening for us to sell for the game today. Keep an eye out for those and don't tell customers that call in beforehand that there will be tickets. That only creates more work for all of us."

The group nodded, knowing they didn't need any more calls to handle.

"Jeremy and Elliott will be leaving us at ten to go work the new outfield bar. You'll all get that chance, so be sure to use them as resources to learn more about what that entails."

Elliott nodded at Jeremy from the opposite corner of the office and grinned.

"Let's have a great morning so we can enjoy the game and festivities this afternoon," Sammy finished, and headed back into his office.

Jeremy turned on his computer, not dreading the phones for once, since he would only need to field calls for two hours. *Hopefully they don't release the tickets until after ten. Then I'm out of here.* He would normally be ready to pounce on the opportunity to buy the Opening Day tickets, but TicketStubs stopped ticket sales three hours before game time, leaving him no time to post and sell seats.

He logged into his phone, and much to his delight no call came ringing through right away.

Ken Hakes, the team's director of ticketing, walked into the call center, passing the three rows of desks and ignoring everyone on his way to Sammy's office. He closed the door to the fish bowl, which always indicated a serious discussion.

Ken overlooked all the sales departments—outbound sales, season tickets, and the call center—and reported directly to Sue Ellen, the VP of ticketing. He had worked for the team since their inaugural season in 1993.

Jeremy glanced over his shoulder and saw Ken's bald head bobbing in conversation. He'd had minimal encounters with Ken, despite his office sitting across the hall from the call center. Ken kept to himself and never started conversations with his staff; instead he'd walk by with his weasel face down to avoid eye contact.

A call came in, and Jeremy answered, missing Ken walking out. Sammy looked more pale than normal as he stared blankly at his computer screen.

Dang. Hope everything's okay, Jeremy thought, assuming he was home free from his own scheme.

"What do you think that was about?" Scott Walker asked. Scott sat in Lewis's desk when Lewis worked his second job as a suite attendant during day games.

"Who knows," Jeremy replied. "It could be anything on a day like today."

With my luck they're not gonna let me go outside today after all.

*****

The rest of Jeremy's short morning dragged on, despite the calls picking up in volume and remaining steady, with a handful waiting in the queue at all times.

The clock finally crawled to a quarter until ten, and Jeremy prepared to mentally check out for the day. Ken entered the call center again and stared at Jeremy as he walked toward Sammy's office.

What the fuck? Jeremy thought. He knew Ken was leading the outdoor bar project, and figured maybe he was trying to familiarize himself with the people who would be working with him.

Ken didn't close Sammy's office doors this time and remained standing as he spoke to Sammy.

Jeremy put his phone into "Not Ready" status, just as he heard his name being called from directly behind him. He spun around in his swivel chair.

"Hey, Ken, how's it going?" Jeremy asked, trying to hide his surprise.

"Hi. Good. Can you walk with me, please?" Ken's manner was short and brusque.

"Okay, sure." Jeremy's hands fumbled as he locked his

computer and he felt his pulse pounding in his temples. He tried to calm himself down. *Must be about working out at the bar today.*

As they walked out of the call center, Jeremy felt his coworkers' eyes glued to him.

"So how has your morning been going?" Ken asked as they passed Kylie, seated at Jeremy's old outbound sales desk, dressed in a pinstriped pant suit with extra makeup caked on her face.

"Good. Busy," Jeremy said as they passed the elevator lobby. His stomach was in knots; he had no clue where they were heading. "Ready to spend the afternoon in the sun."

"Of course," Ken replied, avoiding eye contact. "Should be a good time."

They walked further down the hall, passing the season ticket and group ticket employees.

"This way," Ken said as he turned the corner to the exit door that led to the club-level concourse.

The door swooshed open as Ken led the way. Club-level looked pristine, with its freshly vacuumed purple carpeting and polished wooden panels that ran along the walls. The concourse was deserted, with the exception of a couple of chefs walking by in white uniforms. Jeremy nodded to them.

Ken led them past more elevators, toward a door that led to the press boxes and TV and radio booths. Jeremy had been in there a couple of times before. The area had its own lounge, and special lunches had been served there on occasion.

"Please head in," Ken said, stepping aside to hold the door open.

The lounge was dim except for some lights above a table, shining down like a spotlight. At the table sat Sue Ellen and a man in a gray suit that Jeremy didn't recognize.

"Please have a seat, Jeremy," Sue Ellen said, not looking up from a stack of papers in front of her. Her long, golden hair looked as stiff as bristles on a broom. She wore a purple suit with boxy shoulder pads that made her look uncomfortable. He had only had a handful of encounters with Sue Ellen in the past, mostly small talk in the break room, but never anything work-related.

The man in the suit stood up to reveal his towering height. His face looked flushed and his gray hair was combed over to hide a balding spot.

"Jeremy, my name is George Schmidley," he said, extending a large hand, which Jeremy shook. "I'm from the Major League Baseball offices in New York and was asked by the Bears to do some private investigating. I've worked as a private investigator for many years and have become quite good at it. So please keep that in mind while we ask you some questions this morning."

Jeremy sat down across from Sue Ellen and George, his hands shaking. His heart felt like it was trying to pound its way through his rib cage. *Okay, stay calm. The evidence can't be strong. Multiple cards and names were used. Play dumb.*

"Jeremy, I'm extremely disappointed," Sue Ellen said. "But I need to hear your side of the story."

The light beamed down on him and he realized it created an interrogation atmosphere.

"We want to ask you about some tickets we've come across for sale on TicketStubs. Are you familiar with that website?" George asked, crossing his hands on the table.

"Yes," Jeremy replied, feeling like he might vomit. *Anyone in ticketing knows about that site.*

"Have you ever posted tickets for sale on their website?" Sue Ellen asked.

"No. I've bought concert tickets on there, but have never sold any." Jeremy tried to calm his mind, and rushed through the list of poker tells he'd always used. *Don't gulp. Don't touch your face. Stare them in the eye when you speak. Keep your hands steady.*

How the fuck did they catch me?

"Well, I have reason to believe that isn't true," George said.

"Do the names Tyrone Smith, Heath Miller, and Travis Martin mean anything to you?" Sue Ellen asked.

Holy shit. They got me.

"No, not that I recall," Jeremy said, careful to stare Sue Ellen in the eyes.

"Funny. All three of those 'people' have been purchasing Opening Day tickets and posting them on TicketStubs. And all three have been tied to the same three credit cards." Sue Ellen pursed her lips tight.

"But the common denominator is you," George chimed in. "You were the representative listed on each transaction, ten in all."

"Now would be a good time to come clean, Jeremy," Sue Ellen said. "We know it's you."

Shit.

"Alright, I've been buying Opening Day tickets and reselling them online."

The room dropped silent. George looked disappointed, perhaps expecting a bigger fight. "Why'd you do it?" he asked.

"For the money," Jeremy said, not feeling any better after his confession.

"I'm so disappointed," Sue Ellen said. "After everything

you've been through here."

Jeremy looked down at his hands. *I can't go to jail for this, right? I did nothing against the law. Worst case I get fired.*

"If I could, I would put this on your permanent record," Sue Ellen said. "But lucky for you, there are no laws against what you did, so I can't do that. We are, however, terminating your employment with the Bears, effective immediately. Your two employee tickets for the game today are being voided as well. Mr. Schmidley will escort you to your desk to pack your belongings."

That's it. My dream is out the window.

George stood and walked around the table to meet Jeremy, who stood on legs that felt like gelatin.

"This way, Mr. Heston," George said, extending a hand toward the door.

Jeremy turned to find Ken hiding in the shadows by the door like the coward he was. He avoided eye contact one last time as Jeremy passed him on his way out. George grabbed a box for him to pack his things.

The two walked in silence across the concourse, through the office, and back into a bustling call center, busy with phone calls as first pitch approached, less than three hours away.

Everyone looked at George with curiosity, having never seen him before. He walked Jeremy to his desk and placed the box on top of it. Scott was on a phone call but watched with disbelief as Jeremy pulled down pictures and shoved four years of his life into a small brown box.

"Got everything?" George asked. Jeremy nodded in response, his head hanging low.

As Jeremy followed George out of the call center, he glanced into Sammy's office. Sammy kept his eyes fixated on his computer screen, but the shock on his face was apparent.

Jeremy walked as stealthily as he could, hoping maybe no one else would notice as he walked by clutching a box that clanged with every step. He kept his head down as he passed Kylie's desk and Matt's office for the final time.

The elevator lobby's door swung open, and he walked through the familiar passage as he had done hundreds of times. George called the elevator and patted his leg with his hand while they waited.

I can't believe this. An MLB investigator? For a few scalped tickets? He'd never anticipated such a drastic action and thought back to what he could have done differently.

The same employee account meant it was obvious from the start, but the real clue was the credit card. *My employee account has processed at least 400 transactions since February. They had to have run some sort of report to find duplicate card numbers being used.*

The elevator chimed and the doors parted to show Michelle with a huge grin on her face that vanished the instant she saw Jeremy holding the box.

"Jeremy?" she asked, eyes bulging.

"I'll call you," he replied coldly.

She stepped out of the elevator and moved to the side. George entered and pushed the button that would take them to the main lobby of the stadium. The elevator hummed as it began its decent.

"I know this is a scary situation." George spoke for the first time since leaving the meeting. "But you're young and will be just fine. Make sure you learn something from this mistake."

Jeremy's mind was racing so fast, he could hardly process George's words. But he was cognizant enough to know that

George had showed him more compassion in the past minute than anyone else from the Bears had shown him in his prior four years.

The elevator doors opened to the deserted lobby of Bears Field.

Black tile shined, freshly polished for the new season. The receptionist sat at her enclosed semicircle desk, bright lights shining down on a display case to the right, showing artifacts from the Bears' short history.

George led them across the lobby to the exit. "Best of luck to you, Jeremy," he said, clapping a hand on Jeremy's shoulder.

"Thanks," Jeremy responded, not sure what else to say. He turned his back to push open the doors with his body, and spun around to the outside world.

Hundreds, if not thousands of people crowded the sidewalk along the main street, waiting for the gates to open in an hour. Jeremy realized that he would have to walk all the way around, since his car waited on the opposite end in center field.

Fucking humiliating.

He trudged along Blake Street, pushing his way through the crowd of people with his box. Everyone was too excited to notice him dragging his feet across the stadium.

"Peanuts! Pistachios! Water! Soda!" a street vendor shouted.

"Tickets! Anyone got any tickets to sell?" a scalper chimed in to the mobs of people.

He couldn't help but chuckle at the irony of it all.

Jeremy reached his car, threw his box in the backseat, and cried for the next ten minutes.

*****

"Jamie, you need to turn around," Jeremy said into his cell

phone. She was on her way to the stadium.

"Why?"

"I just got fired and am on my way home. They canceled the tickets that I had left in your name."

"Jeremy." Her voice was a mixture of concern and disappointment, a tone he learned to dread, knowing it usually led to an argument . "What happened? Was it the tickets?"

"Yes. I'll tell you about it later. I'm going to your place now."

As he drove, Jeremy thought back to all the memories he had made during his four seasons with the team. With the stadium in his rearview mirror, he felt a blanket of depression start to cover him. He had attended more than two hundred games during his run and couldn't imagine having to pay to enter the building. He remembered Pray at the Park and his eyes again welled with tears—of anger this time.

I was so damn close.

He arrived at Jamie's apartment to find her car parked in the lot. He parked behind her and jumped out of his car, mind still racing.

Jamie opened the front door of her apartment. Jeremy dragged his feet as he neared her and entered her apartment with nausea building up inside.

"So what happened?" Jamie asked, putting an arm around his shoulders.

Jeremy buried his face in Jamie's embrace and stopped fighting the tears he was holding in.

"It's okay." Jamie tried to soothe him, patting his back and guiding him to the couch. He sobbed, unable to speak.

After a couple of minutes, calming himself down, Jeremy sat on the couch in the living room, eyes puffy and red.

"I just...never saw this coming," he said, his voice flat. "How am I supposed to afford the Chicago trip now with no income?" They had just booked their flight and hotel two nights earlier.

"Stop worrying. I know this is bad, but everything will work out." Jamie stood up in front of him. "It's just time for a new chapter in your life. You can focus on finishing your master's now."

"I suppose," Jeremy said, looking down at the floor. "This is such a shitty feeling. After all I've been through at that fucking place, and they kick me out?" His lips quivered.

"Let's relax this weekend. We can look at inexpensive things to do in Chicago. The expensive stuff is already paid for."

Jeremy nodded, sniffing. "I don't know why I'm so upset. I was *miserable* there." His phone buzzed with an incoming call.

"Who is it?" Jamie asked.

"No one I know," Jeremy said and put the phone back down.

"No. You answer that right now. It could be important."

Jeremy rolled his eyes but obliged Jamie's demand. "Hello?"

"Hello, is this Jeremy?"

"Yes, who's this?"

"Hi, Jeremy, this is Melissa Marsh from E-Nonymous Incorporated. You had applied for a job with us back in January and I was wondering if you might still be interested?"

Jeremy jolted off the couch and stood in the middle of the living room. His arms started to shake as he felt a sudden burst of adrenaline flood his veins.

"Yes. Absolutely," Jeremy replied, trying to hide the excitement in his voice.

"Perfect," the perky recruiter said. "I just have a few questions for you today before we can set up an onsite interview. Do you have about fifteen minutes right now to chat?"

"Of course." *I have all the time in the world, lady.*

"Great. So looking over your résumé, I see you've been over at the Bears for four years, going on five. Can you tell me about some of your job duties there?"

"Yes. My main function is to answer incoming calls, which can range from ticket sales to customer service issues to disgruntled fans wanting to complain about the team. I also did some work with our outbound sales team, running sales reports and printing and preparing their orders for shipment."

"Great. And why would you be looking to leave, if I may ask?"

Jeremy smirked at Jamie, who sat on the couch staring at him in amazement.

"The sports industry is more competitive than you might imagine. You pretty much have to wait for someone to die before a job opens up. And besides, my background is in psychology, which has nothing at all to do with answering phones."

"I see." She sounded like she was on her hundredth call of the day. "Tell me what you know about E-Nonymous."

"Well, I know E-Nonymous helps people in distress—in fighting addictions or any sort of life problems. I've also heard a bit about the company culture you have, and it sounds amazing."

Melissa chuckled. "How is the culture at Bears Field?"

Jeremy paused. "Poisonous. We have no fun. But that's

74

because working for a pro sports team is a perk in itself."

"Interesting. That doesn't sound like fun at all. You're right about our culture—sounds like we're the polar opposite from what you're used to. Our jobs are stressful, so our CEO makes sure we have plenty of ways to blow off steam: ping pong tables, a fully stocked kitchen, weekly massages, and monthly happy hours."

"That sounds incredible," Jeremy said, no longer able to hide the smile in his voice.

"It is. And that's why this is a hard company to join, even though we are relatively new. That being said, if I were to call your manager today, what do you think he would say about you?"

Jeremy grinned, knowing Sammy would rave about him, to ease his guilt at not even saying good-bye. "I think he would tell you that I have a desire to always learn more, and that I'm a 'go to' person for my peers, someone the team can rely on."

"Thanks for sharing. That was my last question for you today. It looks like we'll move forward with an on-site interview. Is there a time next week that might work for you?"

"Well, the team is on the road next week," Jeremy said. "So I can come in anytime, preferably in the afternoon." Jeremy always avoided scheduling morning interviews, since his brain refused to fully function until after eleven.

"Perfect!" the perky voice exclaimed. "Let's plan for Tuesday at two. I'll send you an email with the details."

Jeremy wrapped up the phone call and hung up to find Jamie leaning back on the couch with her arms crossed. "Are you shitting me?" she asked. "Did that really just happen?"

Jeremy noticed his hands trembling. "It did. It's that job I applied for a couple months ago. The new startup. I'm going in Tuesday for an interview."

"See? Just like I say: things happen for a reason. You wouldn't have been able to answer that call if you were at work."

Jeremy sat next to Jamie, resting his head on her shoulder and enjoying the warmth of her breathing on his forehead.

"It's all going to be okay," she reassured him.

"I know. I love you." He smiled, thinking of playing ping pong and drinking at work.

13

Jeremy sat behind the wheel of his car, a 2003 Honda Civic given to him by his mother when he turned sixteen. The cereal in his stomach swirled around like a washing machine as his nerves worked their way throughout his body, causing a slight tremble in his arms and legs.

"Okay. Let's do this," he said in a shaky voice, adjusting his tie in the rearview mirror. He'd had plenty of interviews before, but couldn't recall feeling so anxious. This time was different: he *needed* the job.

His eyes stared back and he noticed the tension in his brow. He took a deep breath and tried relaxing again. "Go in and do great. You have plenty of phone experience, and it's a psych job. You were made for this."

Jeremy stepped out of the car. The sun beat down on him mercilessly, making him more uncomfortable in his three-piece suit. He clenched a black folder holding multiple copies of his résumé in his sweating palm. The parking lot was a never-ending sea of cars, all reflecting the intense sun off their rooftops. He checked the time on his cell phone: 1:45, right on time.

The gray building had windows that stretched the entire length of the facade, but the slightest tint prevented him from seeing inside. The office stood two stories tall, with two large white hands interlocked above the main entrance, the E-Nonymous company logo.

I can't believe I'm actually here. He had always wondered what it would be like to work for a start-up like Google or Facebook. While E-Nonymous was nowhere near those behemoth companies, business experts projected the new psychology technology company would eventually reach a similar status.

The gravel crumbled beneath the slick soles of his dress shoes as he walked toward the building. The office couldn't have been more than a year old.

He climbed the three steps and reached for the glass door, pulling its cool steel handle.

Inside was a whole other story. The door to his left had its window taped with work zone lettered across it. The door on his right had the same fate, and there was not a soul to be seen.

A giggle echoed from above, causing Jeremy to look up toward the open space of the second-floor landing. He couldn't see anyone to match the giggle to, but did notice some stairs to his left that led up to it.

He wiped his clammy palms as he ascended the stairs. The door ahead revealed signage with the E-Nonymous logo and a hand-drawn rendition of the Denver city skyline below it.

Jeremy walked to the door, keeping his shoulders upright in the Superman pose that helped him gain confidence. He pulled on the door knob, but it remained locked.

A petite redhead jumped up from behind the reception desk, and approached the door with a welcoming grin. She pushed open the door, her big blue eyes scanning Jeremy in his suit; he realized he looked out of place in the casual environment.

"Jeremy?" she asked, extending a hand.

"Yes." Jeremy shook her hand, noticing soft skin beneath her fragile grip.

"Welcome, my name is M.K. Anything I can get you before your interview? Water? Soda? Snack?"

"Water, please. That sounds good."

"Of course. Have a seat and I'll get that for you."

M.K. had all the traits one would expect of a young receptionist. She radiated genuine joy, and spoke in a calming yet perky voice. She disappeared around the corner to the break room. All he could see from his lounge seat was a row of circular tables and chairs, where he assumed people sat for lunch.

Jeremy gawked at his surroundings. After four years at the Bears, with their uppity office and business-casual dress code, the relaxed feel at E-Nonymous was a shock.

The back and forth sound of a ping pong game echoed from where M.K. had gone. A handful of people walked in and out, wearing jeans, shorts, T-shirts, and even hats.

This is where I belong, he thought. He'd always dreaded having to dress up for work.

M.K. returned with a full glass of water. "Here you go."

He thanked her and examined the glass. Most places kept a small fridge in their lobby filled with bottles of water. The fact that she brought him a normal glass of what he assumed to be tap water made him feel like he was lounging around his own house.

M.K. returned to her seat, and Jeremy noticed that her name tag showed her official title as "Office Manager." He remembered learning that start-up companies shied away from traditional titles like "receptionist," in an effort to move into a new era of business.

Jeremy gulped down his water, noting the metallic flavor, when a bulky black man and an athletic blond woman approached him from the break room area.

"Jeremy?" the blond asked.

He stood and extended a hand. "Yes."

"It's great to meet you. My name is Terri Sharpe, we spoke on the phone after your first round with our People team." The "People" team was their human resources department.

"Ah, yes. Great meeting you, too." Jeremy felt his grin widen.

"This is Trevor, another manager on the team." Terri gestured to the black man, and they shook hands.

"Pleased to meet you," Trevor said in a deep, smooth voice that reminded Jeremy of a late-night talk show host.

Jeremy felt uncomfortably overdressed. Terri wore a pair of hip-hugging jeans, showing every curve of her toned legs, and a solid white T-shirt with the company logo blown up big. Trevor wore black gym shorts, purple shoes, and an athletic shirt.

"Let's head in here." Trevor gestured toward a door on Jeremy's left. Terri led the way, pushing open the door to reveal a small meeting room. The walls were painted green, and a round table with four chairs was in the center of the room. They each took a seat, Jeremy opposite the two managers.

"So tell us about the Bears," Trevor started. "Such a unique job that not many people get to do."

Don't bash them. Keep it clean.

"The Bears have been a great job to have through college. They provided a flexible schedule that worked around my classes. They gave me two tickets for every game and a parking pass that I could use downtown anytime. The free entertainment was a great perk, but now I'm looking for more of a grown-up job, something steady and permanent."

"And you're still in school for your master's, correct?" Terri asked.

"Yes. My classes are online, and when I have to go to campus I plan it for the evenings, so there won't be any issues with my work schedule."

"That's great. We don't have many master's graduates around here," Trevor said. "Getting that will really open some doors for you, as I'm sure you know."

"I look forward to it," Jeremy said. "I'm actually in an accelerated program, to obtain my Master's degree in less than two years. After that I haven't decided if I want to go for a PhD or open a practice."

"Great to hear," Trevor said, his tone flat.

"As we spoke about on the phone, here at E-Nonymous we're big on our culture," Terri said. "We're not your typical phone counseling company. We do so much more, including a heavy focus on preventative care. We have a growing sales team to sell our services to both individuals and companies. How do you feel you would fit in here?"

They stared at Jeremy. *This is what they really want to know.*

"I've done some research online. Your careers page on the website makes your company sound truly incredible, and the word in some forums seems to confirm it." Jeremy paused, gathering his next train of thought. "I'll be honest. Working here would be a complete culture shock. I've never worked for a company that puts so much stock into its employees, not to mention the comfortable vibes of just being in the office."

Trevor nodded, looking at Terri to see if she had any more

questions. She didn't and opened the floor for any questions Jeremy had. He asked some administrative questions regarding pay and benefits.

"It's been an absolute pleasure meeting you," Terri said with a wide grin that showed polished white teeth.

"Thanks for coming in," Trevor stood, extending a hand. "We'll be in touch."

They walked Jeremy out of the room and toward the main entrance. He noticed M.K. had a pair of headphones on, typing on her computer.

"We'll see you soon," Terri said, patting Jeremy on the shoulder.

"Thank you both so much," Jeremy said as he opened the door and left the office.

The door closed behind him as he made his way to the stairs. As he descended, his instinct told him he would be back in the building soon enough. He had a sense of belonging. *Fate.*

As cliché as it sounded, and as much as he hated it when Jamie told him this, he did believe that everything happened for a reason. Certain doors closed so that others could be opened.

But the Bears door hadn't just been closed—it had been slammed shut in his face. He had been caught off guard, and as a result felt nothing but shock during the process. But as he left his interview with E-Nonymous, he wished he could have ranted to Sue Ellen. He wanted to yell in her face, demean her for allowing such unfair treatment of her staff, slap her across her bitchy face for the years of disgust that had built up working for her.

He realized now just how much he hated his life while working for the Bears. Every day after work he had to have a drink to cope with the depression that tried to take over him.

"If you wake up every day dreading the day ahead, happiness vanishes real quick," his father once told him.

You're my destiny, he thought as he sat in his car staring at the E-Nonymous office building. "You're my next open door. You *have* to be."

14

ne week later

O   The airplane rumbled with turbulence as it started its descent into Chicago's Midway Airport. Jamie took the window seat so she could sleep more comfortably. Jeremy craned his neck to get a view of the never-ending Chicago city skyline. Their flight was scheduled to land at noon.

"Wow," Jeremy gasped. He had traveled outside of Colorado, but Los Angeles was the only other big city he'd seen. The sheer size of Chicago was unlike anything he had seen before. The buildings, parks, and homes that stood against the backdrop of Lake Michigan made it look like its own country.

"Babe, wake up." Jeremy nudged Jamie.

Her eyes fluttered as she came back to consciousness. "What is it?" she asked groggily.

"The city," Jeremy said, nodding toward the window. "It's so damn big."

Jeremy caught a whiff of her melon-scented shampoo as she turned her head to the window. "Looks pretty cool. You ready to explore Chi-town?"

"You know it." The captain crackled over the intercom to announce that the plane would begin its descent into the city.

Jamie grabbed hold of his hand during the bumpy landing.

The fifteen-minute tumble ended with a hard thud as the wheels touched down on Earth again.

They deboarded the plane and navigated through the airport with ease as they obtained their bags from the carousel and followed signs to the train station that would take them to their hotel in the heart of the city. The subway appeared to have lived a long life from the dents and scratches on its metal exterior.

The panels in the train windows flashed LOOP, which would take them into downtown and the Magnificent Mile. Jeremy and Jamie got a seat toward the back of the train, their suitcases in front of them. The rumbling of the tracks beneath them gently rocked all the passengers side-to-side in their seats.

The jungle of skyscrapers appeared through a haze of smog. The Willis Tower stood the tallest, overlooking the rest of the city with its white spire that seemed to reach for outer space. The tracks were elevated above the ground, providing a bird's-eye view of the passing neighborhoods.

"You notice none of these houses have any yards?" Jeremy asked. "It's house on top of house as far as you can see."

"I know, it's crazy," Jamie said. "I guess that's what happens in a big city. You gotta save space somehow."

A couple stops before their arrival at the Loop, the train took a dip into the underground, swallowing its passengers with darkness before the internal lights flickered to life. The first stop in the Loop brought mobs of people crowding the platforms, then stampeding their way into the car, bringing a stale warmth and musty smell of body odor.

The static voice on the intercom announced that their stop was next, and Jeremy gave Jamie a look of *How the fuck do we get out of here?* They couldn't see the door anymore. Jamie took the lead, pushing through the crowd with her suitcase, dragging her boyfriend behind her. They reached the exit just as the doors slid shut behind them, smacking Jeremy's suitcase in the process.

"Holy shit, that was crazy," Jamie said as they gathered themselves on the platform, watching the train rattle away into the tunnel.

"Can you believe those people?" Jeremy said. "No one even made eye contact!"

After navigating through the concourse and up a short flight of stairs, the streets of downtown Chicago welcomed them with the bustle they expected from the nation's third largest city. Awestruck, they rotated around for a panoramic view of their surroundings, as an old man approached them.

"Welcome to Chicago, folks," the old man said. He wore a torn shirt and pants, appearing homeless. He held a cup of coffee steaming from the lid and took a sip, then wiped his scruffy white beard. "Where are you looking to go this fine afternoon?"

Jeremy hesitated. "We're staying at the Hyatt, which way is that?"

"Ah, the Hyatt," the old man crackled. "You're only two blocks away. One that way, then one left will get you there." He pointed east, toward the lake, Jeremy remembered.

"Thank you so much, sir," Jeremy said, starting in that direction.

"Any chance you can spare me a buck for being your first tour guide?"

"Sorry, we literally just got here and haven't even stopped for cash," Jeremy said.

"I can wait for you outside the hotel. They have an ATM inside."

What the fuck? Jeremy wondered.

"Thank you for your help today, but we really gotta be going," Jamie said, grabbing Jeremy by the wrist and pulling him down the sidewalk.

The two hurried along, pushing through the small crowd of people on the sidewalk. Jamie led the way to the Hyatt, and a revolving door welcomed them into the main lobby. They rolled their bags to the registration counter.

"Welcome to the Hyatt. Checking in today?" a scrawny man behind the counter asked. He gathered the required information from Jeremy. "Enjoy your stay in Chicago," he said as he handed Jeremy two keycards. "Take advantage of our concierge service. They know the city like the back of their hand."

Jeremy thanked him and they turned for the elevator. Outside, he caught a glimpse of the homeless man pacing in circles.

They rode the elevator to the seventeenth floor, debating if they should have deep-dish pizza or a lighter meal for dinner. The elevator lobby on the seventeenth floor had five different hallways branching out in different directions from its core.

Their room awaited them at the end of the long hallway. Jamie swiped the key card and Jeremy shoved the heavy door open to reveal sunlight pouring in through the window. A queen bed sat in the middle of the room, with a sofa below the open curtains. A lemony scent filled the air.

"What a view!" Jamie exclaimed from the sofa. From seventeen floors above, the city of Chicago looked like a small village. Jeremy joined her at the window, pressing his forehead against the glass.

"Magnificent," he said, admiring the hundreds of cars that looked like ants on the sidewalk. "I'll be right back, gotta use the bathroom." He headed into the bathroom whistling Frank Sinatra's "My Kind of Town."

He stepped out of the bathroom to find Jamie in bed with the sheets pulled up to her chin. Her gentle hazel eyes invited him to join her. Her clothes were in a neat pile at the foot of the bed.

"I thought we could relax for a bit before exploring the city," she said, pulling the sheets down to reveal her perky breasts. "Care to join me?"

Jeremy undressed in milliseconds and joined her under the covers.

*****

They woke to fading sunlight three hours later.

"Shit, we slept all the way to dinnertime," Jeremy said as he stretched his arms above his head.

"Mm-hmm," Jamie mumbled, not bothered one bit.

They lay in bed for a while, listening to the steady blast of air conditioning pouring out of the vents. Then Jeremy jumped up and threw on his same clothes, while Jamie searched for new dinner attire and powdered on a quick layer of makeup.

"Let's go see what this town is all about," she said happily while fixing the bed sheets.

"Pizza it is then!" Jeremy cried, whipping out his phone to find the best nearby deep-dish spot.

They headed back down the long hallway to the elevator, and by the time they stepped outside, darkness filled the city, bringing with it a glow of ambient light from the towering buildings.

"Chicago at night!" Jeremy shouted. "So damn beautiful."

The energy of the city filled them both with a second wind as they walked down the Magnificent Mile toward their restaurant of choice, Giordano's Pizzeria. The famous pizza joint had red neon lighting and a line of people pouring out front. They pushed their way inside to the hostess stand.

The waiting area had an open bench, where they waited for their table. Jeremy, a lifelong pizza fiend, took a deep inhale to fill his lungs with the heavenly scent of baked dough and cheese.

The restaurant's dozens of tables were covered with red-and-white-checkered tablecloths, and one wall was filled with a line of booths.

Jeremy caught a glimpse of a pie as a waitress passed by: a two-inch-tall crust forming a circle around a pool of marinara sauce. His mouth watered.

The hostess called Jamie's name and directed them to their table. They sat across from each other, leaning in to talk over the constant bustle of the surrounding tables.

"Wanna get the meat-filled pizza?" Jeremy asked, scanning the menu.

"Yeah. Wanna get a drink to celebrate?"

"Sure." Jeremy had planned to keep drinks to a minimum since he had no income, but it was their first night out in a new city.

Their waiter took their order and returned minutes later with a rum and Coke for Jeremy and a Long Island Iced Tea for Jamie.

"To Chicago!" Jamie raised her glass. Jeremy smiled and tapped his glass to hers.

They downed two rounds before the pizza arrived. Pies of

this size took a long time to bake. The waiter brought the deep-dish pan to the table, balancing it on his arm with heat pads, and placed it atop the stand in the center of the table.

"Bon appetit!" he exclaimed as he lifted a slice from the pan with a spatula. Jeremy's eyes bulged as cheese dangled from the slice on its journey to his plate. Sauce covered the top of the pizza, something he'd never seen before. Beneath the sauce, gooey cheese filled the space between two inches of pepperoni, sausage, bacon, and ham.

"Is this for real?" Jamie asked, gawking at her slice.

The waiter took a step back with a sly grin. He knew a first-timer when he saw one. He bowed out of the way, leaving them to it.

Jamie took a fork and knife to the pizza and began cutting off a piece.

"Rookie," Jeremy smirked. He believed pizza should be eaten by hand no matter what. This slice required two fully spread hands.

The first bite exploded flavors in his mouth in a magical combination. He closed his eyes while chewing, savoring every second.

"Fuck me, that's incredible," Jeremy said.

He looked across to Jamie, who was poking her slice with her fork and not appearing impressed.

"What's the matter?" Jeremy asked.

"I wanted mushrooms and bell peppers on it," she said in a lifeless tone. "But no, we got what you wanted like always."

Jesus Christ, he thought. *Here we go.*

"Babe, you didn't say anything when I asked if the meat pizza was alright," Jeremy defended himself.

"No, I did. You just weren't paying attention. I'm so sick of having this conversation all the time!"

What the fuck?

"Well, I'm sorry. Do you want me to ask for something on the side?" Jeremy asked. *No point in arguing with someone who never admits when they're wrong.*

"Nope, it's fine," she snapped. "I'll just enjoy your pizza. It's *so* delicious."

Passive aggressive bitch, he thought. Jeremy was also sick of having these conversations—he was always the bad guy.

"Whatever," Jeremy said and returned to his pizza.

They ate in silence. Jamie managed to keep her lips pursed and her brow drawn even as she ate. Jeremy shook his head, fighting off the knots twisting in his stomach.

"So what do you think of the town?" Jeremy asked. Maybe small talk could lead them back to a normal vibe.

"It's cool," she said flatly. "I thought the people would be rude, but they're pretty chill."

"Right?"

Just like that, the two returned to their pleasant dinner. They laughed and swapped stories and made fun of other people in the restaurant. For the remainder of the night, Jeremy forgot about his unemployment situation and enjoyed himself. Dinner led to more drinks, which led them back to their hotel room, where they made love again to cap off the day.

*****

"Had no idea this was here," Jamie said. "Never even heard of it."

"Me neither, but she is spectacular," Jeremy responded, raising his sunglasses to get a better look at the majestic piece of art.

After a quick continental breakfast at the hotel, they headed for Michigan Avenue, a popular tourist area in downtown Chicago, containing landmarks like the famous Chicago Water Tower, Millennium Park, and the Magnificent Mile.

They approached Pioneer Court. Towering above them stood a statue of Marilyn Monroe in her iconic "flying skirt" pose.

Jeremy gawked up at the thirty-foot statue.

"It says the statue isn't permanent," Jamie said, scrolling on her phone to look up facts on the sculpture, named *Forever Marilyn*. "It travels around the country and has been to California, Jersey, and even Australia."

Jeremy focused on getting a clear shot of Marilyn through his digital camera. "Well, I'm glad we were able to cross paths with her," Jeremy said as his camera clicked. "She was one beautiful woman."

Jeremy's pocket vibrated and he reached in to grab his phone, the 720 area code indicating a call from Denver.

"Hi, Jeremy, this is Melissa from E-Nonymous," a familiar perky voice said. "Is now a good time for you to talk?"

Jeremy shuffled away from the statue, where a group of teenage girls were giggling and screaming for no reason. Jamie gave him a curious look and he smiled and held up a finger to tell her to hold on.

"Yes," Jeremy replied. "Sorry for the background noise. I'm actually in Chicago right now."

"Oh, how fun!" she cried loudly. "I love Chicago, but we can talk about that later. I was calling to offer you the position at E-Nonymous. Your interviews were stellar and we would love for you to join the team!"

Jeremy felt relief flood his soul. "I would love to work at E-Nonymous," Jeremy said, trying to sound composed.

"That's outstanding!" Melissa chirped. "Our next training class will begin on May 7. Does that work with your current schedule?"

"Absolutely!"

Jeremy continued to listen as Melissa covered additional details. Once his offer letter was signed, his health benefits would kick in right away. With 100 percent coverage and no out-of-pocket expense, this was officially the "grown-up" job he'd been wanting. After four years of making a measly nine dollars an hour, he was being offered twelve dollars to start, which would increase to fourteen after thirty days.

The health plan was just the tip of the iceberg. Benefits also included catered lunches, a fully stocked kitchen, monthly happy hours within the office, and generous paid time off. He could feel his future becoming better with each word Melissa spoke.

"We have a passion for keeping our employees happy and proud to work with us," Melissa said. "I hope you feel that vibe right out the gate."

"I could tell from my interview that it's a special place to work."

"Perfect. If you have questions before the seventh, please let me know. Otherwise, have a great time in Chicago!"

Jeremy wished her well and hung up the phone in his trembling hand. *Destiny,* he thought. His heart felt ready to burst out of his chest.

Jamie walked over, and Jeremy looked at her with a big grin.

"I got the job," he said. "I start on the seventh!"

Jamie matched his grin. "I'm so glad, babe!" she cried. "Now we can really celebrate!"

"I know! I'm so *relieved.* And you won't believe the benefits they offer. I have health insurance now!"

"That's great! What do you want to do now?"

"Let's grab a small lunch so we can go out for a fancy dinner tonight. We can dress up." He knew how much Jamie loved getting dolled up for a night out on the town.

"Oh? Fancy, you say?" Jamie couldn't hide her excitement and smiled.

They enjoyed the rest of the day exploring the city. Jeremy's good news created a rejuvenation for their relationship, and their day felt like a first date.

Jeremy stuck to his word and took Jamie for an elegant dinner on the 84th floor of the Hancock Tower, overlooking the city. The view was something out of a postcard. They ate and drank the night away, feeling on top of the world. Jeremy had a new job, Jamie had her boyfriend back, and they had so much to look forward to.

15

ay 2012

MIt was the first day of training and Jeremy had never been so eager for a day of work. He dressed and was out the door in a blur, arriving at 7:30 for an eight o'clock start time. The parking lot was deserted outside of the office building as the morning sun splayed its rays across the facade.

He waited for others to arrive and enter the building, then followed them in. M.K. greeted him, showing him to the training room along with a quick tour of the kitchen: an open space with two large refrigerators and a ping pong table.

M.K. left him in the kitchen to rummage through the cupboards in search of a quick breakfast. He made a mental note of the snacks he came across and settled on a cereal bar and a bottle of orange juice, before returning to the training room.

The front of the room had a pull-down projector screen displaying E-Nonymous' logo. Below the screen was a table with an open laptop and stacks of papers. Two long rows of desks faced the front, with five desktop computers in each row. Name tags were clipped to the tops of each monitor; he saw the one with his name, and took his seat.

A couple others were already seated in the row behind him.

Jeremy nodded and smiled to them as he sat down.

A short Asian man walked in with a pep in his step. "Good morning, everybody," he said energetically. "My name is Jason Tong, and I'll be training you for the next two weeks!"

By Jeremy's judgment, Jason was roughly his age, if not younger. His black hair spiked up like a sea urchin and his eyes scanned the room as he took a sip of coffee from an E-Nonymous thermos.

"I look forward to getting to know all of you!" Jason put his thermos down and circled the room to shake the three newbie's hands.

Jeremy stood to greet him and found that Jason was as short as he was, which was unusual. "Nice to meet you, Jason," he said. "Happy to be here."

"The pleasure is all mine," Jason replied. "Welcome to the team."

As Jason made his rounds, two more people entered the room. "Ah, Peter and Patrick!" Jason hurried over to them. "Great seeing you guys, please take a seat." He gestured to their empty desks.

"Pleasure to be back in training, bud," the one named Patrick said. He plopped down in the chair next to Jeremy. "Hey, bud," he said. "Name's Patrick. You can call me Pat, or whatever you want really."

"Nice to meet you," Jeremy shook his hand. "Do you know Jason already?"

Patrick looked down, scratched his sandy hair, and cracked a smile. He looked up with droopy blue eyes. "Yeah, I know him. I think I'm the only person to get fired then rehired a month later. Gotta love start-ups!"

Patrick noticed the confusion on Jeremy's face. "I started in sales. I sucked. They fired me. Then they call me two weeks ago and offered me this customer service position."

"I see," Jeremy said. He'd never understood how some people could spill their life story to a stranger.

The tall, scrawny man in glasses named Peter shuffled behind Jeremy to take a seat on the other side of Patrick. He sat back and propped his foot across his knee, showing off his hairy legs, his toenails hanging out of his sandals.

Pretty laid-back for the first day, Jeremy thought, hoping he wouldn't have to see too many more pairs of feet up close. He glanced around and noticed that both Patrick and Jason wore sandals. Jason sat on the front desk, legs dangling.

A very tall woman entered the room. She looked like a college basketball player with her slender build and athletic attire. A guy was with her, smiling awkwardly as he passed, keeping his head down as his pale face flushed. He had graying hair, and was definitely the oldest person in the class.

"Alright, everyone. Time for us to get started!" Jason announced. He scanned the room. "I'm Jason, and we're going to become the best of friends over the next two weeks. We'll be meeting in here every morning to go through training on the E-Nonymous products and procedures, legal matters, and of course, how it all ties in to your job. Later this week we'll hit the floor so you can do some call listening with the more experienced reps."

They all nodded.

"Let's get started," Jason continued. "This morning will be all about the company. How we got where we are today and what the future looks like."

Jason held a remote and clicked it to change the slide. The company logo gave way to a big, bold lettered statement: *WE*

DON'T HIRE ASSHOLES!

"First thing to know about E-Nonymous is that we don't hire assholes," Jason said as they all chuckled. "We're more than a company—we're a family. If you put yourself above the good of the team, you likely won't last too long. We can only move our company forward by working together as a finely tuned machine. Besides, our mission is to help people dealing with serious issues, so why would we employ an asshole?"

The morning carried on while they learned of the young company's history and founder, Sami Eger. Sami had come from Norway to study psychology at Stanford. With a master's degree in hand, and a hunger for helping people dealing with suicidal thoughts, addiction, and mental illness, Sami decided to start his own network of fellow psychology students for people to call.

It started as an experiment, to see how many people would utilize such a program. There were already suicide hotlines, quit-smoking lines, and a number for gambling addicts to call. They could all be found running commercials on TV in the middle of the night.

Sami wanted to differentiate his service, to be more appealing. Attending school in the heart of the technology world, Silicon Valley, Sami realized the importance of making it more accessible than the typical hotline. He connected with software engineers on campus, told them his idea, and within two weeks he had a fully functioning mobile phone application called E-Nonymous.

The app incorporated Sami's vision: people across the spectrum could be in touch with an expert with a tap of the finger. The app allowed direct phone calls, emails, and Sami's priority, a live chat option. He knew most people found comfort in hiding behind their screens, to keep their identity confidential. The live chat option addressed that head-on, which meant Sami could save many more lives, by giving those too shy to pick up the phone a means of communication.

It took only four months for word to spread about the new, free app and its unique features. After reaching 100,000 downloads, Sami decided to implement a small fee for users to connect with the team of psychologists. His hope was that the fee would help curb the incoming traffic for his small team, which had grown to twenty psychologists around the country.

His plan worked for a couple of weeks, but popularity grew despite the fee and by the end of month six E-Nonymous had 100,000 *paying* users and had evolved to a fully functioning business.

Sami had no problem connecting with angel investors in the Valley and accepted an offer of eight million dollars in seed funding to help grow the app into an actual business. He had limited knowledge of business, so he hired a friend from Stanford's business school to assume the role of Chief Financial Officer.

E-Nonymous opened their first official office in downtown San Francisco during the summer of 2011. The original team of ten psychologists assumed roles as executives and upper management, along with ten others located across the country. Over the following year, with some wise investments in marketing and engineering, E-Nonymous grew into a juggernaut in the industry and reached five million downloads of the app. This rapid growth led to the need for expansion and Sami decided on Denver for the location of their new sales and service office.

"And that's how we got here today," Jason said.

*****

The remainder of day one's training flew by, after a deep dive into the company's products and service. Jeremy's brain felt fried from the knowledge packed into it after the long day.

He went home that night knowing that he now worked for a company that cared more about its employees than its executives. The feeling was so overwhelming, Jeremy had trouble sleeping that night.

The E-Nonymous mission statement hung on the wall in the kitchen: *Use our intelligence and care to help those in need.* The first week of training moved along, with hours of information to digest, but Jeremy loved every moment of it. He tried to remain a silent sponge, absorbing all the information, but sitting next to Patrick made that difficult.

Patrick was a natural social butterfly, always talking with those around him, and raising good points during group discussions.

"So what do you think, bro?" Patrick asked Jeremy toward the end of their second day together. "Pretty easy job."

"I'd say so," Jeremy said. "Answer the phone, connect people to the doctors, and chat with others on the internet. Doesn't seem too bad."

Jeremy downplayed his passion with Patrick. He looked forward to helping their clients. There was even the chance someone would call in to the main line and need to be talked off the ledge, literally.

"I hope you're all ready to get on the phones this afternoon," Jason said on Wednesday, the third day of training.

They looked at each other in puzzlement, enticing a laugh from Jason.

"I'm kidding!" he cackled. "You'll just be listening, to get an idea how it's done. Come back from lunch prepared and ready to ask questions."

When they returned from lunch, each of the trainees was assigned a current employee they would sit with for the remainder of the afternoon. "Call shadowing is the most important part of your training," Jason said. "This will be your first exposure to your job, so be sure to learn all you can. We'll meet at 3:30 to discuss how it went. Now, head on out to the floor and find your partner."

Jeremy was assigned to Roberta Gonzales. He followed the group out of the training room, through the kitchen, and onto "the floor." Aside from a quick tour around the office on the first day, Jeremy hadn't explored much outside of the kitchen.

Stepping onto the floor and seeing all the desks crammed together with no dividers between them made Jeremy feel at home. Everyone looked so relaxed; some even had their shoes off while they sat back in their chairs, mid-conversation. Nearly everyone was on the phone, creating a loud jumble of noise that spread across the room.

The desks were arranged in small groupings of six, two rows of three facing one another, with a seventh desk on the end, where the managers sat. Jason had mentioned that no one had their own office, regardless of their position. All the rooms surrounding the perimeter were used as meeting spaces. Jeremy noticed the department's director, Shelly Williamson, seated at her desk in the middle of the floor.

That's so cool, he thought, remembering how rarely Sammy came out of his fish bowl at the stadium.

He sought out Roberta's desk, remembering her from a brief introduction in the kitchen. She was the only other older person at the company, likely in her fifties if he had to guess. She looked a bit ill, with pale skin and virtually no flesh around her bone, bruises and gashes spotting her arms and legs. Despite her crypt-keeper appearance, Jeremy found her to be a kind person, after their short conversation in the kitchen.

He found her at an island of desks with her headset on, speaking articulately to the person on the phone.

"Yes, sir, I know that's what you were originally told, but I'm telling you how it really works," she said, shaking her head as she scribbled notes on her pad. She noticed Jeremy, cracked a smile, and waved him over while she wrapped up her call.

Oh, shit. That doesn't sound like a psych call, that's a customer service call.

Roberta concluded her call and pressed her release button angrily to hang up the phone. "That guy was pleasant," she said through clenched teeth. Jeremy watched Roberta fill out a form on her screen.

"After each call we have to fill out a case to track the activity on each account, and our productivity," Roberta explained as the cursor jumped from field to field on the screen. She reached into a drawer beneath her desk and pulled out a second headset, connected the wires into her own, and handed it to Jeremy.

"Here you go," she said. "You'll be able to listen to my calls through here."

The phone rang, flashing green lights. "It's go time," she said, and answered the call.

Over the first hour Jeremy listened to seven calls, back to back, with standard three-minute breaks of wrap up time in between. The calls seemed like standard customer service issues. E-Nonymous made its big money selling packages of their service to corporations. The calls he heard were simple billing or user account questions. He wondered where his psychology background was going to come into play, and asked Roberta if that hour stretch was the norm for her types of calls.

"Yes. We mostly handle account issues. There was a time when we would get emergency calls, but now those get directed to the doctors. Every now and then one will come through, but that's rare."

"I see," Jeremy replied, disappointed he wouldn't have the opportunity to help people, at least to start. He was also growing uneasy at the thought of fielding hundreds of calls with little break in between. At least at the Bears he could count on consistently slow times of the year. During the off season, receiving more than three calls in an entire shift was a busy day.

There's no off season in mental health, he thought.

"You wanna take some calls?" Roberta asked, popping an old french fry into her mouth.

"Sure, why not?" Jeremy said. If it was just plain old customer service, it was no different from handling angry baseball fans.

Roberta wheeled back from her desk to clear the way for Jeremy. "It's all yours," she said with a grin. She handed him her headset and he fit it snugly over his head, positioning the mouth piece to its proper place. "Just take the calls and talk. I'll be right here to walk you through what to do."

Jeremy nodded and clicked to put his phone into ready status. Two minutes passed without an incoming call. He looked around in curiosity, as it appeared everyone else was on the phone.

He caught Kristan, the tall woman, across the room, watching him with a quizzical look on her face. She mouthed, "Are you taking calls?" to which Jeremy returned a proud nod.

The phone finally rang, and he felt his heart sink into his gut. He took a deep breath and answered, "Thank you for calling E-Nonymous, this is Jeremy." He noticed his hand trembling on the mouse as he tried to navigate the cursor, causing it to zigzag across the screen.

He couldn't have asked for a better debut call. The man on the other end had called in to ask about his bill. It proved a simple task, with just a couple clicks to get to the correct screen. The call took all of two minutes before the customer hung up, satisfied.

"Good job!" Roberta said, scooting in to help Jeremy log his call. "You sounded shaky at first, but clearly you know what you're doing."

"Thank you," he replied. "Was that a pretty standard call?"

"For the most part, yes. There will be varying degrees of difficulty; that was on the easier side."

Roberta guided him through filling out his case, and he felt the nerves settle down. The first call was out of the way—before everyone else in the training class.

She may be a bit different, but Roberta just helped me get a leg up, he thought.

Jeremy took four more calls before their time on the floor ended and they trickled back to the training room, where Jason sat at the front desk, hammering away at his laptop.

"So how did it go?" Jason asked once they had all returned.

"Jeremy over here was taking calls already," Kristan said sassily.

"Oh, really?" Jason raised his eyebrows as everyone turned

to Jeremy. "Tell us about it."

"It was good," Jeremy said. "Roberta handed over the headset and let me go at it. I talked with four customers and they were all polite."

"Very nice!" Jason said enthusiastically. "How about everyone else? How did the call listening go?"

They went around the room, each sharing stories of the calls they had listened to. The mood was relaxed as they all laughed and shared their stories, as if they were lifelong friends chatting around the campfire.

Jeremy knew one thing: he would do well at this job. With his experience from the Bears, he had no doubt he would have a long and successful career with E-Nonymous.

16

May 2012

"I'm happy to hear everything is going so well," Dr. Siva said.

Jeremy had finished his first week of training at E-Nonymous and had a meeting planned with Dr. Siva for that Friday evening.

"Yeah, I feel like I'm in a really good position, to use both my customer service skills and the things I'm learning in school."

The bags under Jeremy's eyes showed that the shift from a part-time job to full-time, plus school in the evenings, had started to take its toll. It wasn't just lack of sleep, but also the overwhelming sense of constantly having something to do.

"Do you think you'll stay happy there?" Dr. Siva asked, scribbling notes on a pad of paper. "Say, two years from now?"

"I think so," Jeremy replied. "I mean, the people seem genuine, the stories about the culture seem legit. I can see myself working my way up and being happy."

Dr. Siva's brow rose in a look of surprise. "That's great," Dr. Siva said, without much excitement in his voice. "It really is. Job security is so important, as is being happy in your position. I just don't want to see you lose sight of your goals. I've seen it plenty of times in our industry—someone is on the path, headed for big things, then they get comfortable and lose the drive to reach for those dreams."

"I won't do that," Jeremy said defensively.

"I'm not saying you will, not saying you won't," Dr. Siva said, monotone. "It's just some food for thought. I talk to fifty-year-old people every day who are sick with regret that they didn't at least *try* to do something bigger with their lives than push papers at some office job."

Dr. Siva paused, keeping an expressionless stare at Jeremy while searching for his next words. "I guess my advice is to remember that you only get one attempt at your life. Make sure to never leave a stone unturned."

Jeremy pondered Dr. Siva's words. "I appreciate that, doctor," he said. "I know I can still do something with my life. I also know it'll be easier once I have my master's."

"With all respect, Jeremy, that's nothing but an excuse," Dr. Siva said. "A master's is just a piece of paper. Sure, it may open the door to some new opportunities, but there's still plenty you can do now. I want you to consider something."

Jeremy fidgeted in his seat.

"On average, a typical person knows roughly seven hundred people. Obviously not all are close acquaintances, but they are in the network. If you can truly affect one person—whether it's a belief, or something as simple as introducing new music to them—you have the potential to reach seven hundred people through that one person. It all depends how much you influence them.

"Take politics, for example. One person can share their vision and get a room of a thousand people to also get behind that vision. Those thousand people share that same vision to their networks, and now our original politician has reached *seventy thousand* people with their one message.

"Take that concept and let it snowball, and that's how you get *millions* of people to support you in an election."

Jeremy nodded, unsure if he followed Dr. Siva's message.

"The moral of the story, Jeremy, is to try and make a difference in one person's life and see where that goes. I know you have this grand vision of your own, but it's something that starts on a smaller scale than you might believe."

"I can do that," Jeremy said, suddenly feeling motivated. "I needed that perspective, thank you."

Dr. Siva grinned for the first time that day. "Of course. It's what I'm here for. Now go get to work on how you want to make a difference in the world."

*****

With a new fire kindled within, Jeremy returned home inspired to complete schoolwork on his quiet Friday night. Jamie continued working evenings and rarely had free time. They had to settle for a short phone call each night, but Jeremy was too tired to care that he hadn't seen his girlfriend in a couple weeks.

His latest assignment covered how to identify a sociopath and what goes into the mind of serial killers. He stayed awake past midnight to finish some reading and even looked into the history of serial killers in Denver.

He learned about Vincent Groves, who killed at least a dozen prostitutes over a decade starting in 1979. Groves disposing of all of his victims on the side of I-70 in Arapahoe County, their legs spread open and posed like mannequins.

He also read about Billy Edwin Reid, from the 1980s. Reid used a similar tactic in his own murdering of prostitutes: ditching their bodies in open fields, and sticking a crucifix up their vaginas.

Not much was learned about the psychology of these two men. Groves had died almost two decades ago, and Reid had been rotting away in prison since 2008 after finally being captured. There were some underlining themes behind their madness, as both chose prostitutes as their prey. Reid likely had a religious motivation, hence the crucifix.

"There has to be a way to identify these people before they start killing," Jeremy said to himself before shutting down his computer. "There *has* to be a way."

He fell asleep thinking of all the lives affected by these two men's murders. How could tragedies like these be stopped?

*****

"Wanna go smoke some weed in my car?" Austin Sadowski asked from his desk next to Jeremy's.

"I'll pass," Jeremy said, trying to hide his surprise at the question at nine in the morning.

"No worries, man, I'll meet you back here in fifteen minutes," Austin said.

The two parted ways, and Jeremy went to the kitchen to grab a cereal bar.

It was Monday, the new training class's first official day on the floor. Jeremy was to sit with Austin for at least the first half of the day, to get accustomed to the flow of a typical workday.

When they met at Austin's desk fifteen minutes later, Austin reeked like a skunk and had a hazy look in his eyes. "You ready, bro?" he asked.

"Yeah," Jeremy said, glancing around to see if anyone else noticed the strong stench of Mary Jane. "You can work when you're high?" Jeremy whispered.

Austin, originally from Long Island, barked, "Yeah, buddy!

Welcome to the start-up world. Seventy percent of the company is high, and no one gives a shit as long as work is getting done."

No one in their immediate area paid any attention to Austin's shouting.

"That's cool," Jeremy said. "I can't imagine getting high at work. Doesn't the day feel two weeks long when you're stoned?"

"Nah. Don't kid yourself. They may make this job sound all important and shit, but at the end of the day we're just a customer service team and they're a sales team." He cocked a thumb across the office toward the sales department. "The best way to get through a day on the phones with these fuckers is one puff at a time."

"Yeah, I'm not too thrilled with the customer service." Jeremy said. "I thought we help people in need."

"Bullshit," Austin said flatly. "Even before they made the changes to our call routing, we were nothing more than a glorified phone operator. You won't get to help any of the loonies even if you happened to connect with one."

Austin noticed the disappointment on Jeremy's face. "I know you have the psych background, so you'll get your shot to move up here. I don't, and that's fine. I'm here for the sweet benefits. Just make a good impression, hit your numbers, and kiss the right asses. You'll be out of this department in no time."

Jeremy let the advice sink in, realizing he wasn't as close to helping people as he'd thought. "Thanks for the tip, I'll keep that in mind."

It's okay, Jeremy thought. *I work for a kick-ass company. I'll have my master's in no time and will have my chance. This is a start-up, I can help it grow.*

The work phone rang, interrupting his conversation with himself. He took the call, pushing his thoughts to the back of his mind for the rest of the day.

*****

"How was day one?" Trevor asked. He had pulled Jeremy into the same room they'd sat in for Jeremy's interview. The white walls were bare except for a lone dry-erase board.

"It went well," Jeremy said. "I felt really good on the phone."

"Glad to hear. I know with your experience at the Bears this should be an easy transition. Talking on the phones is always the same, it's just a matter of learning the new content."

"I couldn't agree more," Jeremy replied, smiling.

"You took sixty calls today," Trevor said. "Really good for your first day. I just wanted to thank you for coming out of the gate so hot."

Wow. Jeremy wasn't used to praise for his work.

"Go home, get some rest, and recharge for day two," Trevor said. "Come back ready to roll."

"Thanks, Trevor. I look forward to it."

They stood and wished each other a good night.

17

December 2012

December brought its usual brisk weather to Denver. They hadn't received much snowfall, but temperatures struggled to break thirty.

Jeremy had been surprised to find himself genuinely enjoying his job. "Going to work sure is better when your manager and company care about you," he told Jamie one night over dinner.

He'd also started to splurge a little now that he was earning an extra five dollars per hour. He paid off his credit card debt, moved into a new apartment closer to the office (but further from Jamie), and his online gambling had become more frequent and enjoyable. He'd cut back his alcohol intake to mostly just on weekends, except for the random happy hours in the office.

One morning in December, Jeremy's uncle, Ricky, had invited him to a session at the gun range. Ricky had recently returned from a job in the Middle East. A former Marine, Ricky worked in a secret intelligence group for the U.S. government. He was back home in Denver indefinitely, on an extended hiatus.

He had stayed single throughout his life, afraid to get close to someone while working in life-threatening situations.

Jeremy was the closest he would ever get to having kids, so he often took him to sporting events, on road trips—and recently they'd spent time together with golf and guns.

"Have you shot a rifle yet?" Ricky asked, pulling a hat over his bald head, muscles bulging as he adjusted his glasses.

"No, only pistols," Jeremy replied.

"Well, you're in for a treat today. I brought my M-16 for us to shoot."

Jeremy felt his heart flutter with excitement.

"This bad boy is a monster. Hope you're ready for it," Ricky said with a grin as they jumped out of his truck. He retrieved a long alloy case from the truck's bed before leading the way into the range. Jeremy noticed the NRA bumper sticker on the truck's back window as he followed his uncle.

Typical second amendment nutjob.

Inside, they browsed the firearms covering the walls while Ricky paid for their reservation. The collection included antiques, pistols, and rifles of every sort. More were enclosed beneath the glass-top counters that ran the length of the room.

"Ready?" Ricky asked.

"Let's do it." Jeremy started to feel some anxiety creep in. He had heard stories of beginners like himself shooting high-powered guns and being knocked on their ass from the booming recoil.

Ricky started for the door with the sign above that read RANGE. He led the way down a narrow hallway, the large rifle case swinging from his arm. Ricky took a sharp left into their bay.

"This is us," Ricky said. He splayed open his case along the back wall and pulled out his M16.

The rifle was a matted, smoky black and stretched more than a foot in length. Ricky kept it pointed toward the ground and looked into its scope, grunted, grabbed two magazines of ammunition, and proceeded to the bay.

He placed a pair of red ear protectors over his head, and Jeremy put his on too.

"Okay," Ricky said loudly, smacking in the crescent-shaped magazine. "This is a powerful gun. Just because you can fire many rounds doesn't mean you have to." He spoke seriously. "Stay in control and focus on your target. Watch me first."

Jeremy stepped back while Ricky mounted his position in the bay. He stood broad-shouldered, his body squared in a proper shooting position while the butt of the rifle planted into his right shoulder. His left hand held the body of the gun in front of the magazine, and his right was led by the index finger fitting snug around the trigger. He flicked his thumb to release the safety, drew a long breath followed by a steady exhale, and pressed his eye against the scope.

A flash burst out of the barrel with a *BOOM*. Ricky rocked back in a subtle motion as Jeremy noticed the target swaying from its hinges.

BOOM! BOOM! BOOM! The shots fired out in a steady cadence ten times as Ricky emptied the magazine. With each shot, the target in the distance ricocheted. He lowered the gun and called the target forward.

"Looks like I still got it," he said with a cheesy grin. Ten holes scattered across the inner rings of the target, some overlapping others to make oval-shaped holes.

"Nice shooting, Uncle Ricky!"

"Thanks. Now let's see what you can do." Ricky changed the target paper and sent it back to its position. He loaded a new magazine and left the rifle on the ledge of the bay. "Step on up."

He side-stepped to allow Jeremy in. Jeremy adjusted his earmuffs to ensure their coverage and slid into the bay with trembling hands. He picked up the M16 and felt the instant transfer of power flow from his fingertips into the gun, breathing life into it.

"Okay, remember what I said. Take your time and concentrate on your target."

Jeremy nodded and assumed the same position Ricky had. His uncle remained a couple steps behind him. Jeremy's hand still trembled and it took all his focus to steady it on the smooth steel.

"Is this on my shoulder right?" he asked.

Ricky craned his neck to get a better view. "You got it."

Jeremy lowered his head and placed his right eye to the scope, closing his left eye. The target, though fifty feet away, appeared large thanks to the powerful scope. The crosshairs roamed around the seven rings as he fought to steady on the center. After a few seconds trying to pin down the target, Jeremy felt satisfied that his target was inside the inner black rings.

His hands steadied, and for a moment the world stood still. The sounds of the other guns blasting drowned into a hollow background noise. He could feel his eyes pulsing as they drew into focus on the target. The rifle no longer felt like an object in his hands, but rather an extension of his body.

Jeremy pulled back on the trigger, but it had more resistance than the pistols he had shot before. He kept the pressure down on the trigger and gave it an extra squeeze.

The flash and *BOOM* rang out in unison, and the recoil of

the explosion felt like a nudge on his shoulder. He wavered in balance, not quite losing his footing.

"You're good!" Ricky shouted. "Reposition and refocus on the target."

Jeremy did as instructed, and to his delight he saw a hole on the outermost ring of the target when he looked back into the scope.

He braced himself on the second shot, knowing what to expect, and fired all the remaining rounds.

"Whoa," he whispered to himself after finishing the magazine. Ricky called the target, to find eight holes in total; two were outside of the rings.

"Six of ten, not bad for your first time," Ricky said. "What did you think?"

"This gun is wicked," Jeremy said while he laid it back on the ledge. "How do I get one of these?"

I could come shoot this every week. I felt like God with that gun.

"Well, this is a fully automatic gun. They're around $15,000 and you have to go through mountains of paperwork with the FBI. So you might look at an AR-15, a semi-automatic, which is much easier to get and much cheaper."

"I'll have to look into that. Thanks, Uncle Ricky. That was fun. I'd love to do it again!" Jeremy couldn't contain his giddiness. *I haven't felt that kind of rush since my first poker tournament.*

"You can do one more mag, but we'll have to plan a trip to the cabin if you really wanna open it up."

Ricky instructed him on how to insert the new clip, stepped back, and watched as Jeremy fired ten more rounds.

18

June 2013

Friday afternoon dragged on and on. It didn't help that it was eighty degrees out and not a cloud in the sky. Jeremy wanted to get to his grill and start cooking and drinking to celebrate the weekend.

His anxiety seemed to make the clock go even slower. The week before he had interviewed for a promotion into a team lead position. The interview had been with the three women managers in customer service: Terri, Shelly, and Nicole.

He'd cracked a joke to break the ice.

"Why did the scarecrow get the promotion?" Jeremy asked to three confused looks. "Because he was outstanding at his job!"

Cheesy, he thought. *Cheesy as fuck.*

Terri burst into laughter, always simple and easy to amuse. Her giggling rubbed off on Shelly, who joined her after some resistance. Nicole managed to contain hers, with a tight-lipped grin and her face flushing red.

"Good stuff, Jeremy," Shelly said. As she was the highest-ranking person in the room, her compliment helped Jeremy relax.

They met for an hour, discussing a wide range of topics, from how Jeremy would handle certain scenarios in a position of leadership to his overall performance over the first year of his job. He had the advantage of being one of the team's top three producers over the past twelve months—and that included a three-month ramp-up period where he wasn't expected to handle a typical amount of calls.

Shelly explained that they were looking to fill three team lead positions: two for customer support, and one for the onboarding team. The onboarding team handled new customer accounts and set them up for a successful start with E-Nonymous. Interviews would conclude on Monday, with a final decision expected to be delivered on Friday.

Decision day had arrived and Jeremy awoke with a churning stomach.

What am I supposed to do if I don't get this promotion? The thought of settling further into a standard role as a customer service representative had nagged at him all week. He'd also started to develop doubt about his career path as a psychologist. He'd dropped out of the accelerated program, unable to balance school and work at the same time, and returned to the regular four-year plan.

Can I really sit in an office all day every day and listen to people for the rest of my life?

His inner psychologist tried to analyze his own behavior.

You're just acting like a typical kid in his twenties, unsure what to do with your life, he told himself.

"But that's not true," he said aloud to himself one night at home. "I'm meant for so much more. I can be more than some overpaid shrink."

These internal conversations had become frequent over the past few weeks. He refused to mention such thoughts to Dr. Siva, however, afraid of the lecture on disappointment that would surely follow. When it came to defending the science of psychology, Dr. Siva took matters to the extreme.

I could take my time in school, take some classwork off my plate, and focus on my job.

I could use the opportunity as a stepping stone to propel me into a future in the corporate world.

Working my way to a VP position at a company like this would be plenty. Make some good money, have the power to make decisions, and enjoy coming in to work every day. What could be better?

He'd tried to talk about his dilemma with Jamie, but she didn't understand.

"My whole life I've seen people 'follow the system,'" she told him. "Go to college, get a job, have a family, and work until you're old. It seems to work for most people. I thought you wanted to be more than some regular Joe working a nine-to-five. Now you're saying you want to give up on your dreams and settle?"

You're the one still tossing pizza. Maybe he had accepted the world as it was—but he didn't want to, however, the comfort and security of a steady job was tempting. Regardless of who might be correct, he knew sitting back and waiting for life to pass him would lead him to one day looking back on his life with regret.

I need this promotion. I'm already well liked by my peers and leadership. Just give me my shot to show what I can do!

The clock informed him that 3 p.m. was only ten minutes away. He'd seen a handful of coworkers go into a conference room with Shelly throughout the day, but couldn't read their expressions well enough to know what had happened in there. Shelly always walked out of a meeting laughing, but that was just her own corporate poker face.

A finger tapped his shoulder, causing him to jump in his seat as he snapped out of the internal conversation he'd been having with himself. He spun around and his heart sank at the sight of Shelly's heavy frame standing over him. *Time for the moment of truth.*

"Hey Jeremy, you ready to go have a talk?" she asked, her pointed nose directed down at him.

"Of course!" He jumped from his chair and walked behind her toward one of the conference rooms. As they passed by the onboarding team, where Nicole sat, Shelly tapped her bony shoulder and nodded her head toward the conference room.

Nicole locked her light blue eyes with Jeremy's, brushed back her golden hair, and rose from her desk to join them.

No one else had extra people in their meetings today, Jeremy thought. *Must be a good thing.*

His hands started to sweat at the angst of waiting to hear the news. Of all the applicants, Jeremy had the least experience.

They entered the conference room, Nicole sat down, and Shelly stood at the door to allow Jeremy to enter before closing it. He took a seat with his back facing the window. Shelly and Nicole sat down next to each other and they both stared at him for what felt like an eternity of awkward silence.

"As you know, today is decision day for the team lead positions," Shelly said. "We wanted you to have the weekend to process the decision, whether good or bad."

Nicole nodded in silence and scribbled something on a notepad.

"I'd like to start by thanking you for interviewing and expressing interest in the role," Shelly continued. "We had many qualified candidates and had some hard choices to make."

Oh shit, here it comes. Jeremy felt doubt try to grasp his mind.

"We were really impressed and you became a dark horse candidate for the position," Shelly said slowly.

Just spit it out already!

"I'm happy to offer you the position of team lead for the onboarding team."

"Thank you so much!," Jeremy said excitedly before realizing he would be off to a new team. "So I'm switching to onboarding?"

"Yes," Nicole said. "We're going to grow the onboarding team and feel you would be the best person to help me do that. You'll report directly to me and work as the number two for the team."

They both smiled at him happily.

"I won't let you down, I look forward to working with you," he said to Nicole. "Thank you for this chance."

"I know you won't," Shelly said. "We'll be announcing the new team leads on Monday morning. It will be yourself, Tyrell, and Dominic. I know you are about to take off for the weekend, so we just ask you don't share this with anyone on the floor until we make the announcement."

"Okay," Jeremy said. "Thanks again."

Shelly rose and extended a hand to Jeremy. "I look forward to working more closely with you. Welcome to the team."

Nicole had a wide smile. "See you Monday. We'll talk more then about your new role then."

"Sounds good, have a good weekend," Jeremy said as he let himself out of the room.

He returned to his desk to find he only had a few minutes left of his work week. Tyrell sat at the desk behind Jeremy and couldn't keep the grin off his face as he watched Jeremy walk back with a slight pep in his step.

Tyrell's skin was black as night, but his grin revealed glowing white teeth. He started to bob his head and pointed at Jeremy. "Let's go get some drinks, Jer. Time to celebrate." He kept his voice low. "I already told Dom. He's down."

"Yeah, man, let's roll," Jeremy said as he started packing his backpack. "We going to JD's?"

"You know it." JD's was host to most of the E-Nonymous happy hours as it was only a mile away.

"Cool. I'll see you guys there. Gotta go call the lady and let her know!"

Jeremy left the office and walked out of the building with a sense of accomplishment.

I did it, he thought, and jogged to his car to call Jamie.

19

ctober 2013

O Across the country in South Carolina, a trial was set to begin. A twenty-year-old boy had opened fire on an elementary school. He had killed twelve children and two faculty members before his gun jammed and police apprehended him.

The shooting had occurred three years prior to the trial's opening statement. The defense prepared to defend their client under the insanity plea—if they could prove the defendant had committed the crime in a mentally ill state of mind, he could avoid jail time and be sentenced to time in a psychiatric facility.

Jeremy had filled in Dr. Siva on his new promotion and received his professor's typical unsupportive response before he changed the topic.

"What do you think of this case?" Dr. Siva asked Jeremy in their monthly meeting.

"Honestly, I think it's bullshit," Jeremy said.

"That's where you're wrong," Dr. Siva said matter-of-factly. "While it may seem like an easy way out, it's really not."

"Even if this kid *is* insane, he doesn't deserve to avoid the consequences of his actions."

"Who are you to decide?" Dr. Siva asked, sitting up stiffly in his chair.

"It's the law—you can't kill people. He killed kids, lots of kids. No way should he be able to get away with it."

"Are you religious, Jeremy?"

Jeremy paused, wondering at the relevance of the question.

"Never mind," Dr. Siva said. "The point is that there are thousands of cases of mental illness that go undiagnosed. Mental illness is frowned upon in this country. You'd be surprised how many people have been executed or are rotting in a cell that actually need medical treatment."

"That doesn't take back what they did."

"Look, I'm not condoning this kid's actions, please understand that. I got chills hearing about the scene he left behind. I feel for the families, but that doesn't mean the shooter has a healthy mind."

Jeremy fidgeted in his chair.

"I'd like to ask you to follow this trial. Not as an assignment, but as a chance to gain some valuable insight about a dark topic within our field of study."

Jeremy looked at Dr. Siva, trying to wrap his mind around what he was saying.

"Keep an objective mind," Dr. Siva said. "Put your emotions aside and keep your ears open to the facts. There will be some highly experienced psychologists testifying in defense of this young man. Pay close attention to what they say. Remember, at the end of the day our job is to help people fighting battles within themselves."

"Okay," Jeremy said softly. "I'll follow it."

"Very good. I look forward to us discussing this trial."

Jeremy felt sick to his stomach. The thought of keeping an

open mind to the horrific acts done by this monster made him doubt his future occupation.

One day I could have some loony axe murderer in my office, and I might need to defend them?

"Thank you, Dr. Siva. I look forward to it as well."

Jeremy left his professor's office with more questions than ever.

*****

Two weeks into the trial, Jeremy was starting to see what Dr. Siva meant. The shooter had been virtually abandoned during his adolescent years by his executive parents who were never home. Having minimal human interaction at home led to social anxiety in the outside world, mainly at school.

He had no friends in high school, never went on dates, to dances, or to football games. He hid in the back of the classroom and avoided group discussions.

With no one to turn to, he started to research depression, looking for any means of coping with the stress that had built up over years as an outcast. By his senior year of high school he had started sneaking his mother's antidepressants only to find his depression worsen after using them.

Having suicidal thoughts, he snuck his dad's gun from its hiding place. The investigation found that he had compiled a list of some of the country's most notorious mass shootings. He obsessed over each shooting, taking notes on what he liked and didn't like. After a couple months of research, the shooter made his plan of attack and carried it out.

"In a matter of four months, this kid went from a loner high school student to a notorious monster," Dr. Siva said. "But why? That's what we need to find out. Obviously the absence of parental guidance attributed, but why did he decide that *this* would be a good idea? Was it an event at school? Did he have a fight with his parents? There's always a turning point.

"Thousands of mentally ill people are perfectly fine and living normal lives. It takes something to trigger such a drastic expression of rage. But regardless, that boy needs serious mental assistance. Until we stop putting mentally ill people behind bars and giving them the death penalty, these kinds of stories will continue."

"I honestly can't say I disagree," Jeremy said. "If anyone could have sat down with this kid, they would've been able to see he was suffering."

Dr. Siva sat in a meditative silence, hands folded below his chin.

"I want to challenge you, Jeremy," Dr. Siva said. "Start thinking of ways to address this issue."

"How?" Jeremy asked, stiffening in his chair.

"Change society's way of thinking. That's the challenge. Convince a jury to see a mass murderer as a victim of undiagnosed medical issues instead of as a monster."

"I don't know, Dr. Siva. Sounds like a fool's mission. People are so closed-minded nowadays. Everyone believes what they believe."

"You'd be surprised," Dr. Siva replied. "Just food for thought. I don't expect anyone to save the world over night, just wanted to plant the seed."

"Fair enough. This trial—I'm glad you asked me to follow it. I'm finding myself slightly obsessed with the justice system."

"Well, that's a conversation for another day. Keep up with the trial, and we'll plan on catching up soon."

Jeremy thanked him, wished him a happy weekend, and exited the doctor's office.

Their conversation weighed on his mind for the remainder of the night. He tossed and turned in bed, unable to shake the thought of all the mentally ill people that had been executed in the past.

If I could just get people to understand life from these people's point of view, maybe there would be more understanding.

He thought back to a book he had read in high school called *Black Like Me*. It was an account of a white man that had gone undercover as a black man in the South during the 1960s. He published his experience to show the world how differently black people were treated. He shed a light on the nastiness of society, and people hated it. The author had to move his family to Mexico to flee the death threats.

I need to expose this for the world to see. Maybe I can somehow infiltrate the system, show what's really going on, and report my findings.

Jeremy tried to relax his rambling thoughts, but now that his brain had hold of the idea it wouldn't let go.

I need to get into a psychiatric hospital. I could just admit myself, tell them I'm hearing voices in my head.

He thought it over, dismissed the thought.

It's not the knowingly mentally ill that are the problem. It's the ones who are undiagnosed.

A botched suicide attempt?

He remembered one of his past professors dismissing failed suicide attempts. "If you truly want to end your life, then you will. There's no gray area."

I have to go to court. I have to be sent to the hospital. Sentenced to the hospital.

He finally started to feel drowsy.

I have to kill someone.

20

O ctober 2013

In the morning, Jeremy was terrified about the dark things he'd considered the night before. *I'm just caught up in the trial. I have a good job, a girlfriend I love, and a loving family. Killing someone in the name of science is absurd.* He would need to find another way to expose the flaws in the system, and decided to move his challenge from Dr. Siva to the back burner and focus on work.

"Tyrell and Dom are both stepping down from their lead roles and returning to be regular reps," Nicole told him in their monthly meeting.

It had only been four months since his promotion, and now Jeremy was the only team lead for the entire department.

"Shelly made the decision and asked them to step away from the pressures of the team lead position. It had become obvious they weren't cut out for the job."

"What does this mean for me?" Jeremy asked.

"Well, you look great in the eyes of all the managers. Until we fill their positions, you'll have to be the main resource for the whole department. So get ready to be busy. I know you can handle it."

"I look forward to it."

"Something else I wanted to run by you." Nicole shifted to a more serious tone. "We're going to start attending events as a company. Mental health conferences. And we're looking to send a customer service rep to help out the sales team on the road. Would you be interested in doing these shows, maybe once a quarter?"

"Uh, hell yeah!" Jeremy cried.

"Okay, cool. I thought so. There's a show next month in Chicago. It's a quick two-day trip."

*****

Being the only team lead in the department was a blessing. Jeremy quickly advanced through the ranks.

He enjoyed traveling to conventions to support the field sales team. Soon Jeremy became the dedicated customer service representative for the entire field sales team of about twenty. It nearly doubled his workload, but he was happy to take it on.

Nicole helped him develop into a leader, allowing him to run team meetings and trainings, and even join her for interviews of potential new hires.

Jeremy's closest friend on the onboarding team, Clark, shared with Jeremy that he also wanted to work his way into a leadership position. Clark had a hefty frame, and a reddish beard. He worked quietly and worked to keep the peace in the group, offered his assistance at every opportunity.

"It's all about bullshit, man," Jeremy told him. "Hit your numbers and kiss the right asses."

"It seems wrong," Clark said quietly. "I should be judged by how hard I work, not how well I play the politics game."

"I know, but this is the game, and it's only going to get worse. If we really do go public in a few months, we'll have investors to answer to."

21

ovember 2014

N Sami called for a company-wide meeting via teleconference. Jeremy sat in the back and watched as Sami announced the news.

"Today, I'm humbled and honored to announce that, as a company, we have made it to the top!" Sami shouted. Applause ruptured across the different offices. Screams, whistles, and clapping all poured through the intercom.

"We're headed into our next chapter, and let me tell you, big things are coming," Sami said. Employees murmured amongst themselves. "I don't want anyone worrying about their jobs. Sometimes jobs are cut to make things more appealing for investors, but a decision like that would have already happened if it were going to. Business will continue as usual."

Sami concluded by announcing that a huge party would take place in a month, when he would ring the opening bell on Wall Street for their first day as a public company.

The meeting in the Denver office concluded with cookies and beer.

"Cheers to us!" Jeremy raised his beer can and knocked it against those around him. "We made it. Now there's no looking back."

*****

The month leading up to the IPO brought plenty of change, with a steady flow of media outlets visiting the office to cover stories for the upcoming event. Everyone was reminded to keep their workspaces clean for photo ops.

Sami ordered lunch for the whole company every day prior to his trip to New York City. Jeremy's fears about losing culture as a public company seemed to be unfounded—there were even more lunches, events, and happy hours in the month leading to the IPO than before.

In the midst of the commotion, Jeremy had taken on even more responsibilities. A small class of three new hires were set to begin their training in a couple of weeks, and Shelly asked Jeremy to run the two-week course. And not only did he get to train the new class, one of the new hires was chosen by Jeremy.

Jeremy continued to prove himself in the training class. Not only did he show Shelly and Nicole his capability as a teacher, he discovered a new passion. Training felt natural, and his psychological knowledge helped him communicate effectively with different people. The new hires came out of their two-week session ready to tackle the phones, with a stronger rapport with one another than any class before. Their high-level performance was no accident.

"What did you do in there?" Shelly asked him.

"I did a scavenger hunt," he said. Shelly raised an eyebrow. "I made a scavenger hunt of random facts about everyone on the team. They had to mingle with the team, to learn who to match with each fact. It was a great ice-breaker."

"Well, that's awesome," Shelly said with a big grin. "I'd like to have you do this again. I'll be sure to let you know when we have more new hires."

22

uly 2015

J "Welcome to Open Hands!" Amanda greeted Jeremy
as he walked into the office.

Her greeting caught him off guard. "Good one," he said
sleepily.

Her awkward grin remained. "I'm not kidding," she said,
looking like she was about to laugh or cry, Jeremy couldn't tell
which. "We got bought out by Open Hands. We're merging
companies."

Open Hands was their biggest competitor. They were
founded a year prior to Sami starting his business, and the
two companies, in a sense, grew up together. Open Hands,
however, led the industry, while E-Nonymous came in second,
slowly gaining ground on their nemesis. The two had a sibling-
like rivalry, bashing the other on sales calls to try and beat
them out on deals with potential clients.

Jeremy had even encountered Open Hands staff at conventions, and had noticed that their exhibit space was always
more attractive and bigger. The two companies merging would
be like the Yankees and Red Sox deciding to join forces.

Amanda read the doubt on Jeremy's face and said, "Check
your email if you don't believe me. Sami wrote to the whole
company."

Jeremy walked to his desk, punched in his password, and waited for his email to load. A bold message jumped out in his inbox with the subject line MAJOR ANNOUNCEMENT!

He clicked on the email.

Dear E-Nonymous,

It is with much pleasure that I announce that our company is set to be purchased by Open Hands.

For years we have battled each other for market share, and it's been a fun ride. We have both grown into juggernauts in our industry, and I feel that there is no better time for us to join forces with our former foe.

I have watched us grow, thanks to the hard work and innovation of our team. Combining that with the resources of Open Hands will allow us to grow even more.

I want to thank you all for the hard work you've put in over the years, helping us get to this point in our young history. Never in my wildest dreams did I imagine us becoming this big.

I know you will have plenty of questions about what happens next, and so do I. There will be a company meeting later today with our new CEO, Lloyd Russell. Lloyd has a passion you'll love, and I'm excited about the direction and vision he has for our new company moving forward. Until then, let's keep showing them why they made the right decision to merge with us!

Thank you again,

Sami

Jeremy didn't believe his eyes. He reread the email.

What the fuck is going on? He looked around as his colleagues filed in for the morning, opened their email, and looked around the office like he was, as if they were expecting someone to jump out of the shadows and tell them it was all a prank.

Instead, Shelly walked to the center of the floor, announcing, "Please gather around, everyone. Quickly, please."

Jeremy thought he heard a slight tremble in her voice, and noticed her face was pale. His mind raced.

Are we all getting fired? Why would Sami do this to us? His email did sound like a farewell.

The department gathered in a circle around Shelly.

"Good morning," she said to her staff of forty, all staring at her in wonder. "As you have seen in your email this morning, there is some pretty big news. We have been bought out by Open Hands. This came as a surprise to all of us, and I've been on the phone with HQ trying to learn everything I can.

"I want to assure you that you still have a job. There are no plans to let anyone go. For the short term, business will continue as usual. There's still a mountain of paperwork and federal approval to get through before this becomes 100 percent official. For the time being, we are still E-Nonymous.

"There will be a meeting later this afternoon with the Open Hands CEO, and he'll have a lot more details. Please hold any questions until then, as I only know what I just told you."

"Are we keeping our brand?" Peter asked.

"I don't know, that will be a question for later," Shelly said in a stern voice. "Today will be weird, but let's focus on keeping it as normal as we can. Check your calendars for an invite to the company meeting. We can meet as a team again once we have more information."

Shelly walked back to her desk, leaving the team to go their own ways. The floor hummed with murmurs and an elevated energy.

Nicole pulled Jeremy into a conference room. "You okay?" she asked.

"Yeah. Pretty shocked. Can they just buy us like this?"

"They can. Sami worked out a deal. He sold us for $3.5 *billion.*"

Jeremy's eyes bulged. "Holy shit."

"Yeah. I was reading some business websites this morning. They're saying it's the biggest transaction ever for a tech company."

*****

The company-wide meeting space buzzed with energy. Unlike the IPO announcement, which surged with an excited vibe, this meeting had a mixture of confusion, fear, and panic.

"Rest in peace, E-Nonymous!" someone shouted in the crowded room, receiving a mix of laughter and shouts.

Jeremy took his seat toward the back of the room next to Sylvia, one of his teammates. Sylvia liked to remain as uninvolved as she could at company events, opting to stick with her small team.

"What you think, Jer?" she asked when he sat. "That be some bullshit if we all get fired today."

"I don't think we have to worry about that," he said. "Just from what I've heard, this can be a good thing for us."

"A'ight, if you say so." Sylvia sat back in her chair as the projection screen at the front of the room flickered to life.

"Is this on? Can you hear me, Denver?" a short man asked on the large screen. He paced in quick circles as he held the microphone to his mouth. His comb-over attempted to cover a receding hairline. "Denver, you are joining us here in Seattle with the rest of the Open Hands team, all five hundred of us.

"My name is Lloyd Russell and I'm the CEO of Open Hands. Today has been an eventful day for all of us, and I wanted to be sure to touch base with you all on what the future holds. First off, welcome to the Open Hands family!"

Applause erupted through the speakers from Seattle, with only scattered clapping in the Denver office.

"I like to be as transparent as possible about the direction of our company, so I'd like to share my vision with you. "I want everyone to rest assured that your job is not in danger. We have no plans to cut positions. We need you. We didn't agree to this buyout to make you go away. This is an investment. My vision is for us to move forward as one, and become the biggest resource for those in need around the world."

Applause ruptured in Seattle, and a few more joined in from Denver.

"The plan for the next three months is to learn as much about each other as possible. That way, once everything is approved, we'll be ready to jump in together and get the ball rolling.

"So I ask of you all, let's put the swords down. We no longer have to slander each other. We can now talk each other up, get customers excited, and let them know big things are coming!

"Thank you for your time today. I will be sending out a follow-up email, please feel free to ask me any questions through a direct response. Otherwise, we will plan more meetings over the upcoming weeks, to share the progress we're making."

Lloyd thanked everyone a final time before saying good-bye. The screen flicked off, and the unofficial head of the Denver office—the vice president of sales, Greg Landers—stepped to the front of the room. He grinned with pearly teeth. The ladies around the office often commented on how handsome he was, despite his approaching his sixties. He still had a full head of silver hair, no obvious wrinkles on his face, and high cheekbones.

Greg raised his hands to silence the chatter across the room.

"Thank you all for taking time out of your afternoon," he said, projecting his voice. "We have big things ahead. I ask you to take Lloyd's words to heart. He really is an outstanding leader and we can all learn a lot under his guidance. That being said, let's get back to work and keep doing what we do, kicking ass and taking names!"

This time the whole Denver office cheered, and everyone stood up to work their way out of the room and back to their desks.

*****

A week later, a cloud of uncertainty still hung over the company.

Jeremy didn't have much time to worry about it. As the customer service department's unofficial trainer, he'd been called on to help with some major training over the summer. The merger meant a change in software used across the company that needed to be taught to the entire E-nonymous staff. Fortunately, Nicole had excused him from all of his regular duties.

Jeremy had received special access to use a beta version of new software to try out. For the first time in six years, he didn't have to fight his way through phone calls to hit metrics. He simply had a checklist of tasks to get done, and he worked through the list with confidence.

He felt natural in the classroom, priding himself in making

the training both fun and educational. Shelly sat in on a session each day, enjoying herself in the review games with the rest of the team.

The week of training flew by and when it ended on Friday afternoon, Jeremy felt both relieved and accomplished. Nicole pulled him into a conference room at the end of the day to check in with him.

"How do you feel it went?" she asked.

"Good. It was a draining week, but a lot of fun."

"Good. Sounds like the team enjoyed your training, so good job."

Jeremy noticed Nicole seemed a bit distant. "Everything okay?" he asked.

"Yeah," she said, sounding unenthused. "I need to tell you something. Shelly is posting the trainer job to the public next week." She paused and looked down at her twiddling thumbs.

"Oh...okay. I get to apply for it, right?"

"Yes, but that's not the point. It's so fucking stupid." Her voice raised. "You're already doing the job, and doing damn good too. I tried to talk her into letting you have it. You've earned it." She paused. "But now you have to interview and go through all that bullshit just to get the job you're already doing. Complete waste of time."

"It's fine, Nicki," he said. "It's my job to lose. I'm sure Shelly just wants to go through the process to make it official."

"I know," Nicole said, rolling her eyes. "In better news—where should we go for drinks after work?"

*****

On Monday morning, there was an email from Shelly announcing to the entire Denver office the open trainer position. She encouraged anyone interested to apply, said they planned to fill the position quickly, and provided the link to apply online.

Jeremy had managed to keep negative thoughts from his mind over the weekend about having to apply for his job. The sight of Shelly's email, however, started a small fire within.

This is bullshit. What if some hotshot trainer decides they want to come join a growing company like ours?

He begrudgingly filled out the application on his computer, typing hard on the keyboard and clicking his mouse with authority.

Attach my résumé? Sure, why not? In case you've forgotten what I've been doing around here the last three years.

He clicked submit. Shelly stood at her desk across the office, and Jeremy glared in her direction. The sight of her made him feel anxious now.

An hour later he received an email from the recruiting team to schedule the initial interview with the customer service managers, followed by a final round interview during which he'd lead a training for the managers on a subject of his choosing.

I've worked closely with all the managers and they love me. This should be a cake walk.

23

uly 2015

The day of the interview, Jeremy had more nerves than he expected. A voice inside him kept whispering, *Don't fuck this up.*

His hands were shaking as he drove into work that morning. He wore a brand-new suit purchased for his upcoming interviews. The collar made him feel like he was choking.

"Looking sharp today," Sylvia greeted him.

"Thanks. Hope it's not all for nothing."

"Why you worried, Jer?" she asked. "It's your job. This is just a formality."

"Right. Thanks." *Why does everyone think this is in the bag but me? If it was a sure thing, there wouldn't be an interview.*

When he got to his desk, Nicole looked him up and down and cracked a wide grin. "Big interview today?" she teased. Her attitude had relaxed from her bitterness on Friday.

"Very funny."

"Good luck, I'll see you in there later."

Jeremy spent the next ninety minutes reading news articles on the internet while his leg bounced nervously. He kept his desk in its standing position, knowing he wouldn't be able to sit still for more than two seconds.

"You ready, Jeremy?" Shelly asked, tapping him on the shoulder from behind.

"Let's do it." Jeremy had so much adrenaline pumping through him, he thought it might burst out of his fingertips. He turned and followed Shelly toward the conference room next to her desk.

Once they stepped in and she closed the door behind him, the nerves vanished like they were never there.

"Please have a seat." They sat down across the table from each other. "Thank you for taking time out of your day for this.

"I want to address the elephant in the room. I know you've been doing this job, and many people have asked why I didn't just offer you the position. You're a serious candidate and the front-runner, but I believe that competition brings out the best in people. That's why I posted the job. No disrespect to you. I'm very grateful for all your hard work over the past few months, filling in on an interim basis. That being said, it's my job to ensure the most qualified person is hired for any role in our department. Are you good with that?"

"Yes, of course," Jeremy said in his most professional tone. *Of course not. This is bullshit.*

"Perfect. Now as far as the interview process goes, I've made a change. I'll be your only interview today. Since you've worked closely with all the managers, there's no need to have them come ask questions they already know the answers to. You'll be moving to the next round of interviews next week and we all look forward to your presentation."

"As do I." Confidence had replaced the nerves, and Jeremy felt ready to take on any questions Shelly threw his way.

To his surprise and relief, Shelly tossed him nothing but easy questions. *Is she trying to make sure I get this job?* he wondered. They spoke for only twenty minutes before Shelly opened her calendar to pick a date for his follow-up interview.

"How about one week from today?" she asked.

"Sounds good to me."

"Terrific. Any questions for me?"

Jeremy paused, remembering it was always beneficial to ask at least one question in an interview. "What can I do to make sure I stand out from the competition next week?"

"Great question. We'll be looking at your presentation skills. In training, you need to be able to teach to different styles."

"Okay, that I can do," Jeremy said. "Thanks, Shelly."

"I look forward to next week." She stood and extended her hand, and he shook it, feeling the coolness of her skin.

"Thank you for this opportunity." *Gotta kiss a little ass,* he thought as they walked out of the room, remembering his own words to Clark just a few months back.

*****

The following Wednesday arrived sooner than Jeremy expected. He had stayed busy putting together a slide show for his group interview.

He chose a topic he could train with ease: how to play poker. It felt natural as he built out his training. He would begin by showing the basic rules, hands, and structure of a poker game. After that he would deal cards out to the managers and they'd all play a couple of hands.

Visual and hands-on training. That should do it.

Nicole had let him know there were three finalists interviewing throughout the week, with Jeremy going last.

"You get to leave the final impression, so make sure you rock it!" she said.

A two hour block was placed on his calendar for Wednesday afternoon, immediately after lunch.

Let's go get this job, he thought. He'd spent his lunch break in the conference room, making sure everything was perfect. He brought his headphones with him and listened to some Kendrick Lamar to get him the zone.

He hummed along while organizing stacks of poker chips, shuffling a deck of cards, and running through his presentation with the projection screen.

Perfect. Everything's perfect. He had never felt more prepared for anything.

Jeremy closed his eyes and did some deep breathing, opening his eyes as Shelly entered the room.

"Hi there, Mr. Jeremy," she said, taking a seat. "You ready for us?"

"Sure am," Jeremy said, feeling relieved as Nicole sat in the chair next to him.

"Good. I know we're all looking forward to it. Right, Nicki?"

"Yup." Nicole faked an enthusiastic tone.

The rest of the managers filed in.

"Welcome!" Jeremy said when everyone was in attendance. "Thank you all for joining me. Today we're going to learn how to play poker. We'll start with some basic rules and strategies, and finish by playing a couple hands."

Terri's green eyes grew in excitement and she grinned at Jeremy to show her interest.

Over the next fifteen minutes Jeremy explained the hand rankings of poker, the flow of a typical game, and a few basic betting strategies, like bluffing and check-raising. He felt like his mouth ran on auto-pilot, so his mind could focus on his audience. Around the table, each manager nodded in understanding and looked to be engaged in the content.

"Now let's play!" Jeremy said. He pulled his deck of cards from his pocket and started to shuffle them.

"I'm coming for all your chips, Nicki," Terri said with a giggle. She stroked her chip stack in anticipation.

"Bring it on," Nicole said.

The managers all seemed laidback and comfortable, which he knew would only work in his favor.

They played two hands with Jeremy as the dealer and unofficial adviser. Terri had called him over to ask his opinion on playing her hand.

Shelly won the first hand, making everyone fold with an aggressive bet and Trevor won the second easily with a pair of queens.

Once the laughter and small talk died down, Shelly shifted the attention back to the interview.

"Thank you for an awesome training," she said. "Now we just have a few questions to ask you."

Trevor started. "We all know you've been doing this job for a little bit. What's been your favorite part so far?"

Jeremy responded, "I've found that I enjoy connecting with our new hires from day one. With all the knowledge I've gained working here, it feels good to share that and hopefully make each new hire class come out of training more ready than the one before."

"Why training?" Shelly asked.

"I've been in a customer service role for a long time now—almost seven years, counting back to my time with the Bears. I'm ready for a change, and training has given me the perfect opportunity to have fun while working and contributing to the big picture."

Jeremy saw Shelly raise her eyebrows, suggesting that she was impressed. "Do you have any questions for us?" she asked.

"I honestly don't," Jeremy said. "Just wondering when a decision will be made."

"Of course. We expect to deliver an offer letter on Friday. You're the final interview, so now we'll discuss the candidates and decide who'll be the best fit for us." Shelly nodded as she spoke, and Jeremy caught himself nodding back as he listened.

"Sounds good," Jeremy said.

"In that case, if you wouldn't mind excusing us, we'll start that conversation right now," Shelly said with a kind smile.

"Yes, of course." Jeremy rushed to gather his laptop, cards, and poker chips. "I'll see you guys later." They all thanked him and he pushed his way out of the room.

Outside the conference room, overlooking the empty gaming room, he exhaled, letting his shoulders slouch.

I did it, he thought as he pulled at his tie knot to loosen it. *That's as good an interview I've ever had.*

He knew he had given it his all—left it all on the field, as they say in the sports world. Now he just had to focus on his job for the next couple of days and await a decision on Friday.

*****

When Friday arrived, Jeremy felt a wave of relief. The voice in his head was still trying to get him to submit to its doubt, and Jeremy wanted it to shut the hell up.

I'm gonna get that offer letter and frame it, he told himself, trying to boost his confidence as the day went by with no word. *If I have to wait until the end of the day, that's fine. As long as I know before the weekend.*

Finally, he received the tap on his shoulder.

"Hi there," Shelly said. "You ready to talk?"

"Yes, of course." His nerves found their way right back.

He walked behind Shelly and Nicole joined them en route to the conference room. Shelly and Nicole sat across from him. He noticed Shelly only had a notepad with her, and Nicole had nothing.

His stomach sunk. *No offer letter in sight.*

"I want to thank you again for going through the interview process," Shelly said. "It was a vigorous process for us as well, but I'm happy to say we had three very strong finalists."

Nicole kept her eyes focused on the empty table, avoiding eye contact with Jeremy.

Oh, fuck.

"That being said, we've decided to go in a different direction for the training position."

The words hung in the air and Jeremy wished he could swat them away like flies. He joined Nicole in staring at the table.

"We've extended the offer to Rebecca Koubek. She is Arnie Koubek's wife, and has a long history of working as a corporate trainer."

"You still have your job as our team lead," Nicole said with a slight waver in her voice. She had a death grip on the table's edge.

"Yes, of course," Shelly said. "We're still very pleased with your performance and look forward to you working with Rebecca closely on the training needs for the team."

"Can I ask what the deciding factor was?" Jeremy asked.

"Absolutely," Shelly jumped in, not giving Nicole a chance to speak. "We felt that, while you're a good trainer, you're not quite ready to take on this role, which will eventually grow into its own department. Once Rebecca grows her program and is ready to hire some trainers of her own, I could see you easily stepping into that role." Shelly paused. "We also felt you didn't express much passion for training."

"How so?" Jeremy felt rage bubbling inside, but kept his composure.

"When we asked why you were interested in training, all you talked about was making a change for yourself."

Bullshit. If I wasn't passionate, I wouldn't have applied. He knew he'd talked about the aspects of training he enjoyed. He couldn't hide the look of disgust on his face.

"I know your friends on the team will be upset about this decision, so I'm looking to you to lead by example and welcome and embrace Rebecca," Shelly said. Nicole finally looked Jeremy in the eye, and he could see her sorrow from behind the stare.

"Okay. Will do." His voice came out cold and unrecognizable to himself.

"Thank you." Shelly had kept her voice calm and friendly throughout all the shitty news. "I know this is a tough blow for you. I'm not gonna pretend I don't know that. Just know you're still highly regarded and this just wasn't the perfect fit we look for. Do you have any other questions?"

"No. I don't."

"Go ahead and take a long lunch," Nicole said. "Get out of the building and wrap your head around all of this."

"Thanks, Nicki." He stood from the table, wanting to get out of the room as fast as possible. He left without another word, closing the door behind him.

Jeremy speed-walked across the office toward the back door, which led to the parking lot. The sun beat down on him fiercely and made him gag. He walked to his car, sat down in the driver's seat, and let the tears flow before calling Jamie.

24

ugust 2015

"How are you doing?" Nicole asked. Three weeks had passed since Jeremy received the news of the missed promotion.

"I'm doing alright," he said. "It's been hard to keep myself motivated, but it'll get better."

After the announcement, Jeremy had let himself go. Stubble scattered across his face and he let his hair go scraggly.

"Listen, it's possible this all happened for a reason," Nicole continued. "I have some news I wanted to share with you."

She paused, waiting for Jeremy to look directly at her.

"Trevor is leaving the retention team, and our new VP has asked me to take over."

Jeremy's heart raced. "So what are you saying?" he asked.

Nicole grinned. "I'm saying my position is going to become available very soon."

"Holy shit."

"Yeah. Having been our team lead for more than two years, this has got to be yours. I'll be recommending you as part of my departure from the team. You need to make sure you step up big time during the transition period, because there will be interviews again. It's just the way Open Hands does things."

He hated the thought of going through another interview process. "Does Shelly know?"

"Yes, the announcement will be made on Monday. Next week is Trevor's last, so I'll be leaving the week after to start with retention."

"Wow, this is happening quick."

"Just another way Open Hands does things. They waste no time. Expect to see the job posted next week, and it will be open to both internal and external candidates."

"Guess I'll be redoing my résumé again this weekend."

"Yes, do that. You're a pro now at interviewing with Shelly."

This is the job Nicole has been preparing me for all these years.

*****

The management team wasted no time in making the announcement: Shelly called for a meeting with the department first thing Monday morning.

Trevor announced that this week would be his last, as he planned to finish school and pursue a career in family law. Nicole would manage the retention team in his absence, leaving the onboarding team manager position open.

Once the announcements were made, Nicole pulled the onboarding team into a conference room.

"I'm proud of all of you for building such a fine-tuned machine. Our productivity is at an all-time high, we get more done than the Seattle team, and you should all take a lot of pride in that."

As the team all chimed in about how they would miss Nicole, Jeremy sat in silence. Even though he looked forward to the opportunity, he also felt stunned and sad that Nicole was leaving. She had always been there, looking out for him.

Now I'm alone.

"Next week, once I'm gone, carry on as usual. Jeremy will be here as always, so make sure to lean on him."
*****

I don't fucking believe it.

Jeremy had read the email at least ten times. His pulse throbbed hard in his temples, to the point where he thought his head might actually explode.

"You fucking cunt," he whispered under his breath, staring across the room at Shelly. The urge to walk over to her and put his hands around her throat was overwhelming.

After everything I've done for this place. Unfuckingbelievable.

He reread the email sent from the recruiting team:

Dear Jeremy,

Thank you for your interest in the position of Onboarding Team Manager. At this time we will continue our search in another direction. We are looking for candidates with past managerial experience.

Thank you,

Open Hands Recruiting

Jeremy deleted the email, wanting to not see it anymore. He felt like he might vomit.

So this is it? I get rejected for the training job, and don't even get a chance to interview for the other position I'm already basically doing. Three and a half years and she can't even humor me with a first-round interview.

He checked his schedule to find he had two hours before his next call. He called Jamie from his car. His voice broke as he spoke and his hands shook.

"She couldn't even fucking tell me to my face!" Jeremy gasped for breath. "She had our recruiters send me a generic response!"

"Babe, calm down. It's going to be okay. You still have school to focus on and you can get out of there once you graduate." Jamie kept her voice gentle and calm. Jeremy broke into tears.

"I don't wanna leave here. I love this place."

"I know. But I don't think you have a future there as long as Shelly's around." She sighed. "Listen, babe, I need to get ready for work. Just try not to worry about what you can't control, okay? Maybe I can come over tonight?"

"I'd like that. See you later."

Jeremy sat in his car for a few more minutes, got his breathing under control, and cleared his mind.

Focus on your job. You're still a top performer. That hasn't changed.

He returned to the office ready to push the situation to the back of his thoughts.

I'm just gonna do my job. It's all I can do.

25

August 2015

Jamie poked at her chicken. She'd joined Jeremy for dinner after his long, dramatic day at work. Her eyes drooped, avoiding eye contact with her boyfriend.

"Are you sure you're okay?" Jeremy asked. She had seemed off since she arrived. Jeremy had ranted more about his rejection and Jamie had just nodded, not contributing anything to the conversation.

"I'm okay." Her voice sounded shaky.

"If you say so. How was your day? Couldn't have been worse than mine."

"It was fine."

That's it? Normally, Jamie talked his ear off. Jeremy felt his heart sink, worrying that something was wrong. *I can't take anything else happening right now. Why can't she just support me?*

They finished dinner, not speaking again until Jamie finally cleared her plate.

"I need to talk to you," Jamie said quietly.

Oh, fuck. Those words never led to anything good.

"Okay. What's up?" Jeremy tried to sound calm.

"I'm in a funk," she said. "I feel like I've fallen into the same routine every day. Wake up, go to work, hang out with you. Something just doesn't feel right, and I think it may be our relationship."

Jeremy gulped.

"I think we need some time apart. I need to get myself together. I don't know what I want in life anymore. I know this is the last thing you need to hear today, but I've been putting off this conversation for too long. Haven't you felt it?"

Jeremy's throat was swollen from holding in tears; he had to force it open to speak. "I mean, sure, we've had our ups and downs, but it's nothing we haven't been able to work out before."

"It's not about that. I just don't know if I want to be in a relationship. I'm only 23. I need to take a step back. The further our relationship goes, the more likely it becomes we end up together forever. Right now, the concept of forever terrifies me."

Jeremy slunk down in his chair. "So when you say we need time apart, you mean like less date nights?"

"No, Jeremy. I mean a full-on breakup. No contact."

He couldn't fight the tears anymore.

"I love you," she said. "This is the hardest thing I've ever done." She stretched her hand out to put over Jeremy's across the table. "But something tells me this is right for both of us."

"Please don't leave me. I can't do this." Jeremy's lips quivered as tears fell onto the table. "I have nothing right now. I can't lose you."

Jamie's eyes turned red as she too started crying. He remembered the time he found her on campus after her last breakup. Now she would probably find someone else to comfort her through this one.

"I don't want to do this," she managed between gasps for air. "I have to." She fanned her face with her hands, leaving a streak down both cheeks.

Jeremy jumped out of his chair and went to her. "Jamie, please. We can help each other with our problems. I love you."

"I know, but I need to handle my problems on my own." She pressed her lips to his, and they were salty from the tears. "I love you, Jeremy. Don't forget that. If life brings us back together then we'll know it's our destiny. You're gonna do big things with that big brain of yours, don't let anything hold you back."

She turned and walked toward the door. Her scent trailed behind and Jeremy wished he could hold it in his lungs forever.

"I'll be right here if you change your mind," he said quietly. "You don't have to do this."

She paused, not turning, and said, "I know." She opened the door, and just like that she was gone.

26

September 2015

"Tell me more," Dr. Siva said. They were meeting before their usually scheduled time, as Jeremy needed to vent. He had already filled in Dr. Siva on his breakup with Jamie and his being rejected for the training position.

"Not even a week after, Nicole tells me she's leaving and her job will be open. It immediately gave me all my optimism back. I thought, I can do this job instead. It all seemed like fate at the time."

"You know fate isn't a real thing," Dr. Siva interrupted.

Jeremy just stared at him. "Right. Anyway, then I applied for the manager position, and Shelly rejected me right away. Not even the chance to interview. Can you believe that?"

"What was her reasoning?" Dr. Siva asked.

"That I don't have any experience as a manager! I've been a team lead for two years. Just because the title isn't 'manager' doesn't mean I'm not managing."

"Hmm. Well, have you thought about what you're going to do? Leave? Stay?"

"I plan on staying there until I finish my master's. Then, I don't know."

"Well, I still think you should consider opening your own practice. If you work for yourself you don't have to deal with corporate politics. When you work for someone else, your job is in constant danger. There's no such thing as job security. A CEO can wake up in the morning and decide to lay off an entire company, and no one can do a thing about it. You live in a constant state of mercy to others."

"Never thought of it that way," Jeremy said. For once he felt like Dr. Siva was talking *to* him, not *at* him.

"There's a lot you can do in this world, and corporate America only stunts your growth as a human being. Now, what I really want to talk to you about: the trial."

"I'm so sorry, Dr. Siva," Jeremy said. "I haven't kept up with the trail. My workload piled up, then all the interview preparation on top of homework took up all my time. Last I heard, the jury was set to make their decision."

"It's too bad you missed it—the ending especially. The outcome was as I expected: they found the kid guilty and sentenced him to death. I thought the defense made a strong case for his insanity plea, but the jury didn't think so."

"That's too bad."

"It's tragic. The psychologists they had on the stand were as good as it gets. They argued that the defendant suffered from undetected paranoid schizophrenia for years. This kid used to yell at the wind, and now he's being put to death."

"I still want to make a difference—I've been thinking about what you said. I know there's something I can do to help with mental illness, I just can't figure out what."

"Join me. I'm going to speak with some law offices about working with them on these kinds of cases. If we can make an impact in the courtroom, that's a chance to make lasting change. I would love to get involved in these type of criminal trials."

Jeremy mulled it over. The courtroom idea excited him. He had watched plenty of court TV, and the cases never lacked in action.

We need a big trial with national attention, and mental illness needs to be the main focus of the trial.

He went home and thought over what Dr. Siva had said. He lay in his bed with the light on, his mind racing too much to sleep. He felt like he needed to confront himself about some of the thoughts that had popped into his head lately.

"You're being dramatic," he whispered.

Not really. You've been having violent urges toward Shelly ever since she fucked your future.

And he had. Ever since Shelly had rejected him for the second time, he had felt rage bubbling from his heart to his fingertips and toes. He had never felt this way before.

"It's rage. Madness," he whispered.

He would close his eyes and imagine grabbing Shelly by the head and stomping it into the ground. He loved the way it felt.

He had so much going for him, and she wanted to take it all away.

"I have no future at Open Hands," he barked. His voice echoed in the empty room and he felt relieved to admit what he had refused to believe.

"My only option is psychology." He forced his voice back to its normal tone. "I can figure out the mental illness epidemic. Sometimes you just need to listen to the world."

He leaned over and pulled a composition notebook and pen from the top drawer of his nightstand, and sat up in bed with the notebook in his lap.

He thumbed through the blank pages, feeling a wave of motivation.

I'm doing it. I'm going undercover.

He opened the notebook and started writing:

The Questions?
- What is the meaning of existence?
- What is the meaning of life?
- What is normal? What is insane? What is sanity?

He flipped the page and continued.

We are born, not by choice,
but by our parents choice.
We are raised by our parents
to be the person we become.
We get an education. For what?
To get a job and work for
someone else.

$$Job = \$ \quad \$ = Value$$

$ is needed to live but we
give our life to someone
else to get $

What is a human's value?
Does value effect existence?
Existence is a continuum,
never ending. People come and
go.
Am I less valuable if I
have $1,000,000 or $0?
The meaning of life is to
survive. The goal is to avoid
death.

Innocent people die everyday.
Does someone ever deserve death?
Yes. No.
All are created equal, therefore
one cannot decide another's fate.
A millionaire can't decide a
homeless man's fate, but they do.
Society & politics allow rich to
help poor, but they don't. Why?
Does value go beyond $?

Is a sane man more valuable than an insane man? Is a sane man in the right to decide another man's fate? Sanity is relative, no concrete definition for insanity.
Find the criteria, make a hard definition, save innocent lives.
Insane people kill other people. Fact of life, is it wrong? Depends who you ask.

Why would GOD command his people not to murder yet cower behind free will?

Jeremy snapped his notebook shut after writing this last line. He had never questioned his faith before, and felt immediately guilty.

"What am I doing?" he asked the empty room, lying back on his pillow.

You're going to save innocent people. No matter what it takes. You'll expose the flaws within the system.

*****

He spent his weekend in a daze. A dreamlike feeling consumed him that he couldn't shake. He left his notebook in the nightstand drawer, refusing to touch it again.

No matter how hard he tried, he couldn't shake the thought of killing Shelly. *Am I losing it, or is this normal?*

People joked about killing their boss all the time. There was even a movie called *Horrible Bosses,* about three workers each planning to kill their bosses. But he had to remind himself: people don't *actually* murder their manager.

And that's exactly why I could, and get off on the insanity plea.

On Saturday he opened a search engine and typed in "Legal insanity," but closed his computer before initiating the search. "Can't have a trail online." If he truly planned to see his experiment through to the courts, he'd have to avoid using his home internet. The campus library prompted a specific student login, so that wouldn't work either.

"The Denver Public Library." He had a card, and knew they only required him to swipe his way into the computer lab. The computers were logged in to a general account and nothing was tracked by user.

He threw a hoodie and sweatpants over his pajamas, rushed to his car, and drove to the library.

The computer lab was an enclosed room tucked in the back of the library. Four rows of computers all faced the same direction. Jeremy took a seat in the back row so no one could see his screen. The teenage boy next to him was wearing headphones and bobbing his head, clearly not interested in anything Jeremy was doing.

He opened the search engine and typed "Colorado Insanity" and the autofill suggested "Colorado Insanity Defense Statute," which he clicked on. He clicked the first link available and the webpage provided him with a good start:

The test for insanity in Colorado was that *"a person who suffered from a condition of mind caused by mental disease or defect that prevented the person from forming a culpable mental state that is an essential element of a crime charged."*

He kept reading. Once a defendant enters the plea of not guilty by reason of insanity, he learned, it then becomes the prosecution's burden to prove the sanity of the defendant.

One fact led to another over the course of the afternoon, and Jeremy left the library that evening with a sense of a plan. The biggest obstacle would be not letting even a trace of premeditation remain. It would require private and careful planning to ensure there was no trace of motive or intent. But he could pull it off.

He was all in on his experiment.

The plan would be to prove that mental illness was a valid reason for someone to commit a crime. Mentally ill people should not be held to the same standards as healthy minded individuals. There were real disorders that went untreated every day, and sometimes a person was no longer in control.

Was there an actual experiment he could carry out to prove the effects of mental health and try to change the perception?

Yes.

He could make sure the pieces were in place to show his insanity in the eyes of a jury. And then he could commit a heinous crime.

The crime to commit?

Kill Shelly.

*****

The thought consumed him, excited him. He constantly had to remind himself not to rush. More research needed to be done, and details had to be planned out to perfection.

In studying court cases where the insanity defense had worked, Jeremy noted that, for the most part, the defendants had an instance where they snapped. There were also cases like Ed Gein, who displayed a lifetime of mental instability—obviously anyone cutting flesh off humans to make lampshades had a few screws loose.

Jeremy took to his notebook to compose his plan.

MUST DO LIST

1. Seem as sane as possible.
   Rebuild relationship w/ Shelly
   Can't have ? about hatred
   towards her.

27

September 2015

Shelly hadn't spoken to Jeremy for more than five seconds since she turned him down for the interview. Apparently she realized what an awkward situation she had created.

Things had at least settled down for the team. They remained productive and continued to lean on Jeremy for support as they all watched the interview process take place.

Jeremy did his part to execute his first step, greeting Shelly every time she passed by, often getting a smile from her. Within a few days, she started engaging with him again.

After an interview with a candidate, she walked by Jeremy's desk, shaking her head, and said, "Oh, people these days. Sometimes all you can do is shake your head. Right, Jeremy?"

"That's right," he said, grinning back. "Rough interview?"

"Brutal," she said, and kept waking to her desk.

You should've interviewed me, dumb cunt.

Jeremy slugged his way through the workdays, anxious to get to the library when the day ended. He could get an extra hour of library time during his lunch break, but decided against it as part of his second task:

2. Leave no trace behind.
Don't get asked questions.
Make everything seem routine.

Leaving the office every day for lunch would be against the norm for someone who brought their lunch four out of five days—just the kind of detail that could prove premeditation in a trial.

Instead, Jeremy went to the library after work, when no one knew what his routine looked like. With no girlfriend or roommate, his evenings were truly his. For all his coworkers knew he went home, played video games, and jerked off until bedtime.

He went to the library with a backpack full of books. As far as the librarians knew, he was coming every day to study in peace, not game-planning an insanity plea for a crime that hadn't happened yet.

*****

After two weeks and nearly a hundred hours in the library, Jeremy felt he had a solid plan in place, but there was one glaring problem: no one would give a shit.

His research concluded that of the cases that had succeeded with the insanity plea, none had really stuck with the public. He needed the American public, if not the world, to be involved and to have an interest in the case.

The one case that had gathered any sort of national uproar was when John Hinckley Jr. was sentenced to a mental institute instead of prison, for the attempted assassination of

President Ronald Reagan. But Reagan lived, so when Hinckley was found not guilty by reason of insanity, it didn't have the same effect as it could have had the president passed away. Had that happened, perhaps Jeremy's mission would have already been complete. But this was also in the 1980s, before social media and a hunger to constantly be in the know, so maybe not.

Jeremy took a step back to look at the big picture.

People are murdered every day. We're conditioned to seeing murder on a regular basis.

If Jeremy killed Shelly, he would get nothing more than fifteen minutes of fame on the local nightly news. His mugshot would be all over the internet as past acquaintances talked shit about him. But his face would be a distant memory well before a trial would start.

He needed an audience, a big one. He needed people to feel connected. He thought back to what Dr. Siva had told him.

"Everyone knows an average of 700 people," he said to himself. "The more people you can affect directly, the larger your reach of influence."

Jeremy had two options: kill a high-profile person, or carry out a mass murder.

Killing a high-profile person could prove too difficult. "Who would I even kill? A movie star? Athlete? Politician?"

A mass murder seemed more feasible, but also opened the door to more questions: Where? When? How? Were there other factors to consider in a mass shooting that could influence his goal of winning the insanity plea in court?

He went back to his notebook with hopes of answering some of these questions.

Locations - need to be heavy populated. Maximize as many casualties possible.
Mall? Grocery Store? Outdoor festival? Stadium?

?

Jeremy doodled a question mark, frustrated by his racing mind. He'd felt like he had everything under control when he planned on killing Shelly, and now felt completely helpless. He rubbed his eyes and planted his face into open palms.

"Oh, my God," he whispered, writing with authority below the question mark.

Office

"It's perfect—the best of both worlds."

I can take out Shelly and achieve a mass murder.

"Mentally ill man shoots up office." Jeremy wanted to hear the potential news headline out loud. "The workplace killer. The office slaughter. Jeremy Heston has a killer day at work!"

He giggled at the last one, and returned to the notebook.

When? Regular day at office or an office event? Can I really do this? Kill my friends.... worth it?

Jeremy knew he would have to kill some of his friends and teammates. If he killed everyone but them, his insanity plea flew out the window.

He closed his eyes, drew in deep breaths, and envisioned himself shooting Sylvia.

Sylvia.

His closest confidant at the office. She was a single mother to a promising young boy. Was ruining that boy's life worth all of this? For the sake of psychology?

A tear rolled down his cheek.

"I have to do it. There's too many people suffering and rotting away in prison."

Jeremy tried to take a step back, to see objectively.

He started a new list.

Plan

Office = Shelly & more

Mass shooting = max casualties
and media attention

Bombs? = distracting & powerful

Nearest police station ≈ 3 mi.
≈ 5 min response time

Can block 2 entrances
Can plant 2 bombs near the
locked doors where people will
run. Side door MUST be blocked

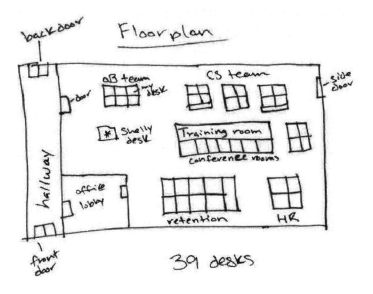

Floor plan

backdoor

door

aB team
my desk

CS team

side door

Shelly desk

Training room

conference rooms

hallway

office lobby

retention

HR

front door

39 desks

- Block side door
- Enter from hallway door
* Shoot from the door, no one will approach
* Shoot Shelly first, she's closest!
- bomb in lobby?

Jeremy closed his notebook, hands shaking.

My team would be the first to go.

He cried himself to sleep, dreamless and deep.

*****

When Jeremy awoke Monday morning, he had managed to clear his mind of his experiment.

It would be absurd to shoot all of his coworkers. They'd done nothing to deserve such a fate.

His conscience cleared once he arrived at the office and he felt the sick feeling in his stomach, which had become all too familiar.

I fucking hate this place, he thought as he placed his backpack under his desk.

Shelly stood at her desk. *Good-for-nothing bitch. How does someone so awful get into such a position of power?*

Jeremy hadn't planned on visiting the library that evening. In fact, he hadn't planned on going back at all. His plan was complete; he just needed to decide if he actually wanted to do it.

You could never.

Shelly left her desk and started for Jeremy, her over-sized ass jiggling with each step.

"Jeremy, can I have a word?"

"Sure." He followed Shelly to a conference room as she chattered on about the beautiful morning. They entered the room and she closed the door behind her while Jeremy pulled out a chair. She sat across the table from him and crossed her hands on the table.

"We need to talk," she said. "I know there's some tension and you're unhappy."

Jeremy felt his scalp tingle as rage instantly boiled up.

He kept his voice calm, despite feeling like he could turn her face into a living punching bag. "I'm okay, it's just been hard to bounce back from the rejection. You rejected me for the training job, then didn't let me interview for the job that Nicole was grooming me for."

"We had strict requirements for the position."

Please. Clark? Clark is at my desk twenty times a day with questions, but he is miraculously qualified?

"Look, I understand you're upset. Why didn't you speak to me sooner about this?"

Me? Why didn't you tell me to my face? All I got was a generic email response, like I'm some bum off the streets.

Jeremy looked down, trying to think of what to say but coming up with nothing.

"Look, Jeremy. I had a decision to make and I stand by it. I'm sorry if it was not handled in an appropriate fashion."

"Fair enough." Jeremy didn't feel the need to beat the dead horse any further.

"I'm hoping we can put this behind us and move forward. And that brings me to what I really wanted to talk about with you."

Jeremy nodded at her to proceed.

"I have hired our next manager. His name is Mark Fernandez. He'll be starting on Wednesday. Now, I know you don't like this, but I'm hoping I can count on you to welcome Mark to the team. The rest of the team still looks to you, and how you handle the hiring of your new manager will affect the rest of the team's attitude as well. So can I count on you?"

"Of course." Jeremy had no intention of making life hard for the new manager, and was offended that Shelly had brought it up.

"Good. Let's make this a smooth transition for everyone. You're still our team lead, don't forget that. Things will work out, they always do."

Easy for you to say.

"I look forward to meeting Mark and working with him to continue our team's high performance." Jeremy had perfected the craft of bullshitting in the corporate world.

Translation: *Fuck Mark. Fuck you. And fuck this place.*

28

eptember 2015

Wednesday brought the person that would forever change Jeremy's life: Mark Fernandez.

Mark walked into the office: tall and skinny, with a demanding presence. Mark's youthful face stood out, and the thought of working for someone younger than him irked Jeremy to a new level. He could see Mark laughing with Shelly at her desk.

Shelly walked over to the team. "Hey gang, let's meet in the training room real quick."

She walked with Mark around the corner, and held the door open as the rest of the team joined. Mark leaned against the front wall, smiling and nodding at each of them as they took their seats.

"Team, this is Mark, your new manager. Mark, tell the team a little about yourself?"

"Absolutely," he said, pushing himself off the wall. "I'm coming over from Marriott hotels, where I managed the events team for the last five years. When I saw the opportunity to join a tech company, I figured it would be a perfect fit."

Jeremy watched Mark, noting that his crooked nose looked like he may have taken a couple punches to the face. His brown eyes rested below a protruding brow. He wore khaki slacks and a button-up flannel shirt.

Give the preppy boy a week before he's in jeans and a T-shirt.

"I look forward to working with all of you. Shelly has filled me in on what an awesome team you've built here, and my goal is to help you all grow even further."

"How about you all introduce yourselves to Mark. Jeremy, start us off?" Shelly asked.

Jeremy nodded from his seat. "I'm Jeremy. I've been with the company for four and a half years, and have been the team lead for the last couple of those years. Welcome."

"Nice to meet you, Jeremy." Mark walked to the front of the table and extended a hand. As he shook it Jeremy could see Shelly behind Mark, smiling to herself.

The team shared more about themselves, as did Mark. He talked about his vision for the team, which sounded like nothing but big talk for a guy who knew nothing about how things worked around here. The team voiced their concerns about things they would like to see improved, and Mark vowed to make those matters a top priority.

They all left the meeting energetic and excited for what the future held—all except Jeremy. When he returned to his desk, he felt squeamish. Mark seemed like an okay hire, but Jeremy didn't see anything particularly special about him.

*****

As Mark settled into his role, the team continued to flourish. Their bonding seemed to strengthen to an ultimate high, but no thanks to Mark.

In fact, it was *in spite of* Mark.

There had not been a team-building event since Nicole had left, so Jeremy arranged a game night at his apartment with the team. Mark declined the invitation due to prior engagements, but everyone else was available and excited.

In typical fashion for their team gatherings outside of the office, alcohol flowed from start to finish. Elayna showed up with a case of beer, Janae with tequila, and Mimi with a bottle of whiskey.

"Let's get fucked up!" Elayna barked as she put the cans of beer inside Jeremy's fridge.

Jeremy set out snacks and finger foods on his counter, and his team wasted no time making plates.

Mimi poured a shot of whiskey for her and Sylvia. They'd became best friends after Mimi joined the team a year prior. The only black girls on the team, they had a natural bond.

Jeremy turned on some music, then made his own plate. Everyone made their way to the living room, sitting on the couch or the floor. He had cleaned up this space, where he spent every evening eating take-out, and even vacuumed the carpet, knowing his mother would be proud.

"Guys, I'm so sick of Mark. He always wants to meet up," Mimi said. "Like, just leave me alone and let me do my job."

"Ugh, I know, it's so annoying," Janae whined.

Jeremy shot a glance at Elayna. They had discussed how Mark clearly favored Janae. She was attractive and charming, and he had more private meetings with her than the others, and always called on her to do special favors around the office.

Elayna rolled her eyes when Janae looked away, making Jeremy grin.

"We can talk about anything in the world, and you wanna talk about work?" Jeremy asked.

"Damn straight," Mimi replied. "I don't get to say these things at the office, and gotta sit there and let it boil up.

Mark's a fool. He tried changing our schedule to work all sorts of fucked-up hours. He can never answer a question, he *always* changes the subject. He's a dumbass."

"Our team is so lame now," Elayna said. "With Nicole, it was like we could come do our job, have fun, and just kick it. Mark is so intense, it's like there's either no fun, or all he wants to do is party."

Everyone nodded. "He's crazy, like an alcoholic," Sylvia chimed in. "I went with him Friday after his first week. He had about six shots, four beers, and was a hot mess. He told me he didn't know what the hell he was doing in a tech company. Then he went on about his daddy issues. It got really weird."

"On that note, let's take a team shot." Jeremy went to the kitchen and grabbed the tequila bottle, along with a stack of shot glasses.

After everyone had their shot in hand, Clark raised his. "To our team."

The girls all cheered and everyone clinked their glasses together.

The night proceeded with more and more shots, and while the conversation strayed away from work, it kept coming back to Mark and Shelly, and how they had created such an unpleasant working atmosphere.

Little did anyone realize, it would be their last night together before things changed forever.

*****

Monday morning brought its usual grogginess for the team. Since they were all roughly the same age—in their 20s mostly—they all had similar weekends. Friday and Saturday nights were for partying, Sunday was for recovering, and Monday could go fuck itself.

One of the schedule changes Mark had implemented was to move the team's weekly meeting to first thing on Monday mornings. He seemed to have no reasoning for it, seemed to have done it just for the sake of change.

Jeremy felt extra tired and depressed and could see the same look on the faces of his teammates.

Shelly kicked off the meeting with information on the monthly bonus incentives for the team, along with data on their prior month's performance, her voice like nails on a chalkboard. Jeremy noticed that he was not the only one struggling to pay attention. It was like now that they had voiced their frustrations about Mark together, no one could pretend to care.

As the day progressed, they joked and laughed with one another like any other work day—until Shelly started pulling everyone into meetings, one by one.

Janae went in first, followed by Elayna, Mimi, Cherie, and Sylvia. Jeremy was pulled in last. He had noticed the serious look on everyone's faces as they came out of their quick ten-minute meetings with Shelly.

She approached Jeremy with a fake smile. "Let's go have a chat." She didn't even wait for him to stand up before turning and walking to the conference room. She was already seated once he entered the room, so he closed the door behind him.

"Have a seat." Her tone was harsh and unpleasant. She cut right to the chase. "What the hell are you doing?"

"I'm sorry?"

"Don't play dumb with me. I know what happened. Everyone on the team has told me."

"I don't know what you're talking about."

Shelly shook her head in disgust.

"You had a party Friday night at your house with the team." She paused and looked at him, as if to let him say something in his defense.

"Yeah? We all got together to hang out. Not sure why this is news, we've done it before."

"Well, it's news because you let the conversation turn into a giant bitch-fest about Mark."

"That's not at all what happened. People were having conversations about all kinds of different things. Did I hear Mark's name mentioned a couple times throughout the night? Sure. But that's normal."

"The fact is, you had a team gathering at your house and everyone felt compelled to complain about Mark. You allowed it to happen."

"Believe me, the last thing I wanted to talk about was work, but that's where people kept taking the conversation."

Shelly paused to draw in a deep breath. She made no attempt to hide her disgust toward Jeremy. "If you want to be a leader, whether at this company or elsewhere, you can't be getting involved in petty behavior like this. You have to change that conversation right away. Nip it in the bud."

Elsewhere? Jeremy felt the rage bloom up in him again. His leg bounced out of control beneath the table. "Understood."

"I don't think you do understand. You were in that meeting this morning. There was an obvious black cloud hanging over the team. No one gave a shit what Mark had to say. That much was clear. Mark felt bad, and that's why I started to ask around."

"Look, Shelly, I'm sorry this happened. But I honestly don't feel like you should be pinning it on me. I didn't even participate in the negative talk."

Shelly slumped her shoulders. "Whether that's true or not, it's not the point. You're at a crossroads. I suggest you take the right road. I don't want to ever have this conversation again."

Shelly stood and walked out of the room.

"What the fuck?" he whispered to himself.

Is this bitch for real? Did my team just throw me under the bus to cover their own asses?

Jeremy knew it was human nature. People rarely stood up to authority, looked them in the face, and admitted their faults. Especially when they had an out.

He doubted any of them intended to do such a thing, but their explanation of the night's events painted that scenario in Shelly's eyes. He sunk his head into his palms, closed his eyes, and a picture of the plan he'd conceived entered his mind, crowding out all else.

It's time to revisit the notebook.

29

November 2015

Jeremy returned to the library over the weekend. He was ready to move forward with his experiment. He grabbed a computer at the end of the row, for privacy.

His initial search began with "Colorado Gun Laws" and it yielded quick results that improved his spirits.

"The state of Colorado prohibits gun registration [CRS 29-11.7-102]."

Check.

"Colorado allows a person to carry a firearm in a vehicle, either loaded or unloaded. Handguns (ones with barrels under twelve inches) are allowed in homes, businesses, or cars, as long as they're not concealed [CRS18-12-105(2)]."

Check.

"Thank God for the NRA," he whispered under his breath. All Jeremy needed to do to obtain his weapon of choice was pass a background check—which would be a breeze, with nothing more than a couple of parking tickets on his record.

He set out on a search for which gun to buy. His uncle's M-16 weighed on his mind. While he couldn't buy the military-issued firearm, he could buy one like it. When he searched for which AR-15 to purchase, there were hundreds of results. Prices ranged from as low as $120 to well above $1,000. He read reviews, and advice from experts.

An hour of research led him to the Smith & Wesson M&P15 assault rifle. Reviewers raved about its performance and light weight. The matted black color of the gun looked polished to perfection.

It's beautiful.

The price tag of $700 was also beautiful, another one of the reasons customers raved about it. He had the money to buy it right now.

This will be the only paper trail I can afford to have. They'll run a background check, and there will be online records of the transaction. Ammo I can buy in person with cash. I'll need to let some time pass between the purchase and the plan. Can't let it seem obvious.

He checked his calendar. November 22.

March? Should be enough time to practice and get acquainted with my new toy.

He sat back and looked at the computer screen, the button to buy looming.

Will this hold up in court? Can this be seen as premeditation, or could I still appear insane?

He thought back to the cases he had studied. How the gun was obtained was never relevant to the case. If a mentally ill person meant to do harm, they would get their hands on a gun one way or another.

Jeremy pulled out his credit card, entered the info. His purchase needed to be shipped to a local firearms dealer, so he chose the one nearest his house: Mile High Armory.

He provided his social security number for the background check, and his home address. The confirmation screen told him that the Mile High Armory would contact him as soon as his order arrived at their store, in about a week.

That's it? He stared at the confirmation in amazement. It was that easy to buy a machine that could help him kill dozens of people in a matter of seconds?

He logged out of the computer and packed up his backpack to leave. As always, no one paid him any attention.

This would be his final trip to the library. The research was done, the gun purchased, and there was nothing left to do but wait: for March, when he planned to carry out his plan and change the face of mental health forever.

*****

The gun arrived promptly on November 29, a Saturday. He missed the call, but the employee from Mile High Armory left a message informing Jeremy was free to pick up his purchase at any time.

He saw the voicemail flashing on his phone, dropped what he was doing, and headed for the Mile High Armory, just a five-minute drive away.

Nerves started to rattle their way into his gut. He wasn't sure why he felt anxious. Could his conscience be trying to throw him off his plan?

This thing is bigger than me. I'm gonna change the world and help people. His reassurance had started to sound like a broken record, even to himself.

People buy guns every day. Just be cool, act normal. Don't stand out as a nervous person, the clerk might recall that later.

He arrived at the storefront, a nondescript building with a plain sign that showed the company's name. It was in a strip mall, surrounded by a nail salon and a Mexican restaurant. The handful of people shopping and minding their own business put Jeremy at ease.

"See, nothing to worry about. Just doing normal, everyday

shit. I'm gonna go and get my gun, then maybe grab a taco next door. Totally normal." He spoke to himself before killing his engine and getting out of the car.

The stench of rubbing alcohol from the salon next door stung his nostrils as he approached the gun store. He noticed a small NRA sticker on the door, similar to the one on his uncle's truck.

A bell chimed when he pulled open the door, and he walked into a nearly deserted store. A man in a cowboy hat stood in the far corner of the room, holding up two scopes side by side, peering into each of them. The clerk behind the counter looked up from a book he was reading. He wore thick-framed glasses that were black like his slicked-back hair.

"Good afternoon, sir," he greeted. Jeremy had assumed that gun shop owners and employees all spoke like country folk, so he was surprised when the man's accent sounded no different than his own.

"Good afternoon," Jeremy said, approaching the counter. He extended a hand to the employee. "My name is Jeremy Heston. I believe you called me about an hour ago for a pickup."

"Ah yes, Mr. Heston," the man said, returning the hand-shake. "My name is Charlie, and yes, your order has arrived. Let me go to the back and grab it. If you could get your ID out for me that would be great."

Charlie the gun dealer. Jeremy took a mental picture of the man, knowing he would likely see him in court in a year or so.

Charlie went to the back and returned seconds later with a large brown box about a yard long. He placed it on the counter and patted the top. "Your ID please, and we can open her up."

Jeremy handed his driver's license to Charlie, who held it

up and looked at it from every angle to make sure the water marks underneath the plastic were legit.

"Thank you, Mr. Heston. Now let's take a look at what you got here." Charlie pulled out a switchblade and cut down the seam of tape. He opened the flaps and pulled out a black case that housed the rifle. He pushed the case toward Jeremy.

"Would you like to do the honors?" Charlie asked him.

"Yes, thank you." Jeremy flipped up the clasps that held the case closed, letting it pop open a couple inches as he glanced over his shoulder. He lifted the lid all the way back, revealing his rifle and its beautiful glow from the fluorescent lights above.

Charlie whistled. "She's something else. When you gonna take her out to the range?"

"Hopefully tomorrow," Jeremy replied mindlessly. He ran his fingers over the rifle, feeling its cool steel beneath his fingertips. His eyes bulged in amazement at how big the rifle looked despite its light weight.

"Am I good to go?" he asked, still not breaking his trance.

"Yes sir. Just need you to sign that you received this fine firearm today. Let me lock her up for you."

Charlie pushed over a piece of paper, closed the lid, and snapped the clasps shut. Jeremy signed where needed and pushed the paper back.

"You're all set. I threw your copy of the receipt inside the case for you."

"Thank you, Charlie, you've been a big help."

"Pleasure is all mine. You need any ammo or anything?"

"Not today. Pretty sure my uncle has some extra he wants to give me."

"Fair enough. Well, then, have a great time with your new

baby there. Look forward to seeing you in the future."

You have no idea.

Jeremy nodded, and grabbed the case off the counter. It hung down to his knees, but felt no heavier than a book. He focused on walking at a normal pace out of the store despite wanting to break into a sprint to his car. He noticed no one in close proximity and walked to his car, rifle case banging against his thigh with each step.

See, totally normal. No one cares.

He felt instant relief. It reminded him of his first time inside a marijuana dispensary. He had been nervous to enter, and wondered what the big deal was when he left. Was there someone from the morality police sitting outside dispensaries and gun shops waiting to see who goes in and out? Of course not.

He tucked his case underneath some blankets in his trunk. His mind raced, still in the grips of the adrenaline rush.

Where am I going?

That God-like feeling had consumed him again. He had a weapon that could kill dozens of people in seconds in the trunk of his car, and no one knew. It made Jeremy want to go to Shelly's house and shoot her on the spot, but he knew he needed to clear his mind and stick to some sort of plan.

He would buy some ammunition and take his new "baby" to the shooting range.

He sat in his car and spoke to himself. "Just go home. Make a schedule for visits to the shooting range, and buy the ammo tomorrow."

Jeremy did just that. Everything was in place now.

30

D ecember 2015
Two weeks passed, and Jeremy still hadn't paid a visit to the shooting range. In fact, he'd decided against it. Becoming a regular at a shooting range was a terrible idea. If anyone started to notice his visits, his whole plan would go to shit.

He would need to practice his shooting in private—make trips to the mountains, find some deserted space, and set up targets. His uncle had property in the middle of nowhere, but it was at least a two-hour drive with no traffic to get there. Jeremy would need to make it work.

He drew up a rough calendar in the notebook, starting from December and running through the end of March. He'd never been much of a planner, but he wanted to plot out each day for the rest of his time in civilization, knowing he may likely never see freedom again.

The company holiday party was set for the following weekend. Lloyd was flying every single employee to Seattle for a company-wide meeting on Friday, followed by an elegant party in the Washington State Convention Center. Jeremy would fly out Thursday night and return Sunday afternoon.

He considered taking his new toy with him to Seattle and shooting it at a range up there. No one there would remember him and his quick weekend visit, but he figured coworkers would likely ask to hang out, pulling him away from any potential free time he might have.

Jeremy circled every Saturday following the holiday party, stopping on March 5. That gave him two and a half months to familiarize himself with the rifle. He drew a star over March 11.

Setting a date made the whole thing feel suddenly real. There was a schedule to follow.

He'd need to make the most out of each visit to the mountains. He planned to leave the apartment at eight in the morning, arrive by ten, shoot for two or three hours, and be back home by four at the latest.

Still have my evenings free.

Jeremy grinned a relaxed smile. Everything else would take a back seat to his experiment. He felt inspired for the first time in months. He knew the reason for his existence, and couldn't wait to share it with the rest of the world.

*****

The morning of the holiday party started at eight with a team meeting in the company office, a forty-story skyscraper overlooking both downtown Seattle and Elliott Bay. Everyone enjoyed meeting one another in person for the first time, and Shelly gave a phony speech about how much she loved all her new co-workers, calling them the best team she had ever worked with.

Jeremy had believed that the struggles of life in the corporate world were the same in any business or company. His belief was confirmed when he met Joey Dreher.

He had worked with Joey and communicated with him over chat and emails, but meeting him in person showed Jeremy the truth. Joey's experience at Open Hands practically mirrored that of Jeremy's time at E-Nonymous. Joey even looked like Jeremy: short, light-skinned, thin, with brown hair.

Joey had worked with the company for four years. He grew into a leader and earned the title of a senior account manager, the equivalent of E-Nonymous' team lead. He had mastered every aspect of his position and more, only to be passed up for numerous promotions.

Joey told his story to Jeremy as the team walked to the convention center for their company awards show and meeting. The two hung back, chatting. They'd had an instant connection.

"Do you ever think about just leaving it all?" Jeremy asked. "Just quit, say fuck you, corporate America, and go sell candy on the beaches in Mexico?"

"I'm sure those people are happy and not stressing about some bullshit every second of the day." Joey shook his head. "None of it makes sense to me at the end of the day. We go to school, get degrees, get a job, and work our way up to pay off those degrees. It seems like the most backward shit. You work your ass off—for what?"

"Just hoping someone else likes you enough to help your career," Jeremy cut in. "You never have real control. It's all smoke and mirrors." He paused, thinking about how much to say. "I'm looking into other options. Working for myself."

"What are you thinking?"

"I can always open my own practice. Help people. I'd rather get into research though. I've got some theories I'd like to try and prove. Maybe I should look for a job as a college professor. They pay you to go out and do research in your field. Could be perfect."

"I'm sure the politics are just as bad, though, working in education. You'd still be shackled by the college dean and their agenda."

"True. I just feel like my time is up here. I've hit my ceiling and there's nowhere to go now but down."

"I know exactly how you feel. How much you wanna bet all the awards today go to the biggest ass-kissers in the company?"

*****

The award show was massive. The room was bigger than a football field, and tables filled the space in front of the stage, which stood elevated at the front of the room. Lunch was served and the show started promptly at noon, with Lloyd as the emcee.

The first half-hour consisted of Lloyd's usual speed-talking, reviewing the company's numbers for the year and the vision going into next year. It had been the company's highest-performing year. Stock prices trended upward and Lloyd expected nothing but continued growth.

After his presentation, every manager in the company lined up at the side of the stage. Each would present an award for their best performer. Shelly stood ten back in line, and Jeremy waited as the first nine announced their winners.

Maybe I could win. I'm sure I was at least considered. He hated that he still cared.

Finally Shelly stepped up to the podium and adjusted the microphone to her level.

"The account management team has gone through so much change this year. It's had its ups and downs, and while the whole team has kept the pedal to the metal, one person stood out from the rest. Janae Ortiz, come on down!"

Jeremy rolled his eyes. "Predictable," he said to himself as the room flooded with applause. Jeremy watched Janae walk onstage to hug Shelly, receive her glass trophy, and return to her seat—and he watched Mark watch her the whole way too.

Jeremy felt the familiar anger boil up yet again. Shelly had her way of ruining his day whether she meant to or not. He watched her walk offstage to return to her table.

I'm taking you first. You're part of the experiment, but you're for me.

He imagined it, *felt* it. Pulling the trigger on Shelly would feel liberating. He daydreamed about it for the remainder of the show, not bothering to hide his bulging erection.

*****

Jeremy cleared his mind after the show. He had four hours before the holiday party started, plenty of time to change clothes and grab dinner before heading over. While he normally wouldn't show up to a party at its start time, this one had an open bar, and he intended to get as drunk as possible.

All his friends had planned dinner with their significant others. They invited him to join, but he didn't want to deal with the awkwardness. *Maybe I can find a random sales girl at the party to hang out with later and possibly hook up with at the end of the night. This could be my last chance at anything casual.*

Jeremy changed into his suit after a couple shots of rum, and went to a burger joint. He sat at a corner table overlooking the restaurant and noticed some familiar faces from the company, but no one he knew on a first name basis. He watched a basketball game on the TV above his table while he ate his burger and fries. His buzz hit, and it felt great. He felt loose, clear-headed, and ready for a long night of partying.

He paid his tab around 6:45 and left for the convention

center. The night was young in downtown Seattle, and many people were starting their night out. Groups of people passed Jeremy and paid him no attention, laughing at one another's lame jokes and hogging all the space on the sidewalk. A light drizzle started, and people took shelter under building overhangs, clearing the sidewalk for Jeremy. When he arrived at the convention center, his suit jacket was a darker gray from the moisture.

The building was warm. He rode the escalators up to the grand terrace and saw the party as soon as he arrived at the top.

A line for the coat check wrapped its way down a hallway. Photo booths were set up everywhere, and photographers were snapping Open Hands employees posed in front of giant snowflakes towering in the background. Fake snow fell from the ceiling onto the main entrance, creating an indoor winter wonderland.

Holy shit. Jeremy had been to plenty of holiday parties with 400 people or so, and had always thought of those as large events—but this made those seem like mere gatherings. Lloyd had said 1,500 people were expected thanks to the two companies merging.

An archway above the entrance read "Welcome to the Open Hands holiday party!" in human-size letters. He looked around and saw no familiar faces.

An usher greeted him and handed him a map of the venue. *A map?! How big is this party?* The map showed the venue divided into three sections: the main dance floor, a karaoke room, and a silent disco.

The main dance floor was straight ahead. Crystal chande-liers hung from the ceiling, and the room was lit only by the flashing lights that moved to the beat of the booming dance music. Between Jeremy and the dance floor stood a circular island with eight bartenders inside it. Lines had started to form in front of each bartender.

Jeremy felt his mouth drool and walked to the shortest line he could find. He saw Shelly standing around the other side of the bar. *Cunt.* He felt his stomach cartwheel at the sight of her, knowing he would need to avoid her at all costs to ensure a pleasant evening.

The line moved quickly, and soon Jeremy's bartender was cracking jokes with him while she poured two rum and Cokes. "Make sure you come back and see me." She winked at him as she pushed his free drinks across the bar. He tipped her five dollars and began his search for anyone he might know.

He had taken his eye off Shelly for one minute while he spoke with the bartender, and she had made her way around the bar and was now directly in his path. Their eyes locked; he was going to have to talk to her.

"Jeremy, how are you?" Shelly asked him. A fat bald man stood behind her, sipping a cup of wine.

"Doing good, how are you?"

"Hanging in there. This is quite the party, huh?"

"Indeed."

"Have you met my husband? This is Chuck."

She stepped aside and Chuck stepped up, extending a hand. "Nice to meet you, Jeremy. I've heard lots about you."

I'm sure you have.

"Pleasure is all mine, Chuck." Jeremy returned a firm handshake. "I was just about to go find our team. Have you seen anyone yet?"

"Not yet. I'm sure I'll see you later."

"Sounds good, enjoy the party!"

Because the next holiday party you'll be nothing but a distant memory.

Jeremy felt like he was reading from a script. But he was relieved to have gotten the encounter out of the way. Now he could go back to enjoying his night. Jeremy had always been able to separate himself from reality. Sure, he would be shooting his teammates in a few months, but that didn't stop him from enjoying their company at the party.

He got to see all of his team at one point or another in the evening. Clark was mostly with his wife in the karaoke room, Janae and Cherie at the bar, Elayna at the silent disco, Mimi and Sylvia at a table near the dance floor. Mark wandered around looking for people to take shots with.

Mark and Jeremy drank roughly the same amount of alcohol, but Mark was nearly twice Jeremy's size—he still had some composure by the end of the night. Jeremy, on the other hand, was sloppy, his world spinning. The DJ played "Don't Stop Believin'" to end the night.

Is this the only fucking song DJ's play to end a party?

Everyone filtered out, retrieving their jackets and taking final pictures in front of the giant snowflakes. Mark stood near the escalator, apparently waiting for someone. Jeremy walked up to him.

"Good party, eh?" He patted Mark on the back, and felt that his suit jacket was drenched in sweat.

"Hell of a time. Can't believe they actually flew us all out here for this. So legit."

"Right? Not bad for your first holiday party with the company."

"Not bad at all. Can I ask you a question?"

"Okay?"

"Be totally honest with me." He was slurring his words slightly. "Are you cool with me? Like, I know you're professional and all in the office, but are we good?"

I'm way too drunk to be having this conversation right now. Jeremy realized this, but he didn't care.

"Yes, Mark, we're good." Mark didn't seem to notice Jeremy's dismissive tone.

"Right on. I know this is a shitty situation for you. I went through the same thing once. Just keep grinding and you'll get where you're supposed to be."

Motherfucker, I'm older than you. Don't try to preach wisdom at me.

"I know. I look forward to working with you and growing more." Jeremy had learned, thanks to his many years in customer service, how to stroke the ego of assholes.

"That's what I like to hear. We can make a great team. Like what I've heard about you and Nicole. How do you think the team feels about me?"

Jeremy paused, but decided, *Fuck it. We're all going down in a few months anyway.*

"Honestly...the team is a bit flustered by all the changes you're trying to implement. Like you're trying to do too much at once. I understand you want to prove yourself, but maybe dial it back a bit?" Jeremy used the most polite voice he could muster. The last thing he needed was friction between himself and Mark—that would not look good in court.

Mark nodded, keeping his eyes to the floor. "Thanks for that. I appreciate the honesty. I really should get going, though. We can talk about this more back at home."

He turned and walked off and down the escalators.

"Fucking asshole," Jeremy said once he was gone.   He reflected back to this moment as a key turning point in events that now had him pondering every single detail that led up to his current placement in jail.

31

December 19, 2015

Jeremy jumped out of bed an hour before his alarm went off Saturday morning, and was on the road by seven. He'd been waiting, ever since his return from Seattle, for Saturday to arrive. His first day of taking his new toy out for a spin.

He drove into the mountains, on unpaved windy roads, into a small town called Sheephorn, a community of cabins used seasonally for hunting and camping. His uncle's cabin stood at the bottom of a hill, surrounded by hundreds of trees that eventually opened into a clearing of flat land where Jeremy planned to set up his target practice. The closest cabin belonged to the Wells family, roughly a mile away. Jeremy hoped no one would be there, and saw no cars parked in front when he passed it.

Jeremy wouldn't be able to go inside his uncle's cabin, as he didn't have a key—but he didn't need to. He parked his car, jumped out, and retrieved his black case from the trunk. The fresh mountain air filled his lungs, giving him the energetic boost it always did. Birds sang from the tall trees, but otherwise the mountain was dead silent.

Jeremy put his case on the hood of the car, unsnapped the clasps, and flipped back its cover. The AR-15 seemed to glow in the bright sunlight.

He brushed a hand over the gun, rubbing its barrel and trigger. "Let's change the world."

He grabbed the bag containing his ammunition and targets, which he'd purchased with cash earlier in the week. The hundred-pack of shooting targets and thousand-pack of bullets would surely last him his couple months of training.

He pulled out the targets and a couple boxes of ammunition. He had twelve training sessions planned, and figured he would practice about a hundred rounds each time. He'd need to purchase more for the actual event. The boxes thudded on his hood where he tossed them.

Jeremy planned to shoot from the cabin area. He looked around for trees that were roughly thirty to forty yards away. He wouldn't need to shoot further than thirty yards in the office, so he'd decided to practice inside of this range.

He picked a couple trees, taped his targets to them, and ran back to his car. "It's time." He panted as he opened the box of ammunition and started to slide each round into the magazine. The bullets sparkled with their golden coat, each roughly the size of Jeremy's index finger. They looked like miniature rocket ships, with their pointed tips and wide bodies. The brass felt cool underneath his fingertips.

He noticed a slight tremble in his hands. The excitement had been building up for a while now. Having the gun sit idle for two weeks had driven Jeremy more mad with each passing day. The time had finally arrived.

With the magazine loaded, he picked up his loaded gun for the first time. Its light weight surprised him again. Even fully loaded, it felt like he was holding a two-liter bottle of soda, not a weapon that would help him change the course of history.

He pulled back on the rifle's charging handle, and there was an authoritative *CLICK!* as the first round was loaded into the chamber. He turned off the weapon's safety with a quick flick of his finger. He couldn't wait any longer.

He raised his rifle and pointed toward the targets. He could feel the blood and a rush of adrenaline bursting its way into his fingertips, which rested on the smooth steel of the hand guard. His right hand fastened around the pistol grip and his index finger found its place on the trigger.

Don't forget the kickback on this bad boy. He remembered his uncle's advice.

He steadied his arms and lowered his eye to the rifle's scope. The silhouette on the target sheet wavered with even the slightest movement that Jeremy made. He placed his target on the center of the man's chest, took a deep breath, and squeezed the trigger.

The shot rang out and echoed around the mountain, causing birds to flutter from their trees. It sounded like a car backfiring. His shot missed the target and clipped the man's shoulder, where the black of his body met the white of the paper. As for the recoil, it was no worse than someone poking Jeremy just below his collarbone—but it had been strong enough to move him completely off target.

This time, he wasted no time pulling the trigger. Then again. And again. He did this ten times, until the magazine emptied. The spent shells were scattered on the dirt below him.

As he practiced, he mentally planned his attack. *I walk in to the office. Shelly is at her desk, facing away from me. I poke her in the back with the gun and pull the trigger as soon as she turns around. People start screaming and running like headless chickens. I aim, focus, and pull the trigger until the screaming stops.*

Jeremy walked to his target on the tree. Three had hit the man's chest, one hit his head, three more hit the paper, and three were unaccounted for, probably stuck in another nearby tree.

Not bad for the first time. He'd shot pistols plenty of times before and was pleased to find that the rifle learning curve wouldn't be as steep as he'd feared.

He reloaded his magazine with ten fresh rounds, realizing he would need to buy more magazines. In his research, he'd found that the state of Colorado prohibited the use of magazines that held more than ten rounds. Other states didn't have the same law, and he was sure one of the neighboring conservative states would sell him a thirty-round magazine.

Jeremy took his time shooting the remaining ninety rounds in his practice for the day. He improved with each round, and felt much more comfortable by the end of the day. He had the kickback under control and now felt his mission would be easier than he had envisioned.

I could do this next week. I feel ready.

His favorite part of it all was the powerful feeling he had with each pull of the trigger. The adrenaline didn't wear off until he fired his last round of the day. He felt one with his rifle; by the end of his practice session the rifle felt like an extension of his body.

I need to stick to the plan. The timeline is perfect—rushing into things only makes the probability for mistakes greater. And one mistake could cost me my life.

Jeremy couldn't recall a time he'd had so much fun shooting. He knew it would take some time to master, but using his own AR-15 was truly special. He wondered what would happen to his gun if he was arrested and eventually released on the insanity plea. It would sit in evidence for a bit, but once he was deemed an innocent man, would it be returned?

For now, he could only focus on one thing: practice, practice, practice.

*****

Jeremy's day-to-day life soon became immersed in his experiment, until it was hard to tell one from the other. He would go into work, do enough to get by and remain unnoticed, then go home to plan and dream about March 11. His experiment gained power in his mind, demanding his full attention, overtaking the constant reminder that he would be ending the lives of people he truly cared for.

The only time his mind cleared was over the Christmas holiday, which he spent with his parents. They wanted to hear all about school and the job and how life was for their little Jer Bear. As far as he could recall, those things were all going just fine. His winter semester had wrapped up the week before Christmas, leaving his work nights free to dream. And plan. He also enjoyed the break from Dr. Siva, not wanting his mentor to have any insight into his master plan. Spring semester would be a joke as he knew he would be leaving only two months in.

The work days went by in a flash. After years of trying to improve himself every day at the office, Jeremy no longer gave a shit about his future with the company, and it was a relief. But he still needed to stay employed, in order to carry out his experiment. Shooting up his office after being fired would appear too much like vengeance and be a sure ticket to a guilty verdict.

*****

Going into his fourth week of practice in the mountains,

Jeremy nearly had his rifle under control. He practiced hitting his targets in rapid succession, and successfully connected at a high rate. His self-control slipped away when he went to his uncle's cabin. He would start shooting and not want to stop. On one visit he fired more than three hundred rounds, pushing his rifle to its limit as it heated up underneath his hands. That was also useful information: how many rounds it could fire in a short period of time.

Jeremy started to hold his rifle every night, wanting to make it as much a part of him as possible. For fun, he would pull the trigger as many times possible in sixty seconds, keeping track of how much faster he became over time. He averaged around seventy "shots" by the time his index finger had strengthened into what felt like a piece of stone.

Jeremy thought his rifle needed a name, and struggled to find the right one—until one night when a modern-day King Kong movie came on TV.

"King Kong. It's perfect." He stroked his rifle as he said it in a trance. "King Kong fucks shit up, just like you will."

He patted the gun and put it in its case with the care of a parent laying an infant down for sleep.

32

anuary 8, 2016

J When Jeremy wasn't talking to his rifle, he was trying to keep his cool and not strangle Shelly. The year had given way to 2016. New calendars hung around the office, and Jeremy felt giddy seeing them, knowing it was only two flips of the page until March. He wondered what the weather would be like that day. March was as predictable as a wild jungle cat. It could be ten below and blizzarding, or 75 and sunny.

January 8 was Jeremy's birthday. It would be his last birthday in civilization for a while, but he didn't care to make it extra special. He normally took off the day from work and spent it up at the casinos, but gambling required concentration he simply didn't have anymore, so he opted to keep the day normal, go to work, and meet his parents for dinner in the evening. Being a Friday, he could plan to make a trip to the casinos if he still had the itch on Saturday morning.

The morning started off like any other. He made a couple calls, played some ping pong with Clark and Elayna, and even treated himself to doughnuts for breakfast. When eleven o'clock rolled around, Jeremy had free time on his calendar and decided to make a quick run to the auto parts store down the street. He had been meaning to get some power steering fluid for his creaking car, as the last thing he needed was to run into any car troubles as March approached.

He bought the fluid, filled it up under the hood, and was back in the office a half-hour later. When he returned, Mark saw him and walked away frantically to Shelly's desk.

What's his deal?

Jeremy's relationship with Mark hadn't improved, or worsened. They understood their situation and accepted it. They could work together just fine, but Jeremy wasn't going to be inviting him out for drinks afterward.

Jeremy logged back into his computer and was checking his email when he saw Mark reappear with Shelly. He held a chocolate cake decorated with Batman figurines, "Happy Birthday Jeremy!" written on top in blue.

"Happy birthday to you!" Mark started the song, and the rest of the team joined in, singing as they gathered around Jeremy's desk. They all applauded after the song and Mark placed the cake on his desk, along with a knife.

"Thank you all. I could use some chocolate right about now." Jeremy started cutting the cake when reality sunk in again. *This is the last time I'll be eating birthday cake. I don't think they give a shit about your birthday in jail.* "I haven't worked on my birthday in a while. Thanks for making it special."

"Of course, man. I hope you have an awesome weekend and get to relax a bit." Mark smiled as he spoke, but Jeremy sensed that something wasn't quite right. Shelly returned to her desk, not hanging around for cake.

Jeremy didn't concern himself with whatever was happening with Shelly and Mark. They always seemed to be up to something, with plenty of closed-door meetings. But Jeremy knew that Shelly fed on drama, to help herself feel relevant.

"A lot of the higher-ups in Seattle wonder what she does

all day." Nicole had told him this over drinks one evening after work. No matter how distant Jeremy felt, Nicole always brought him back to Earth. She was a true friend, and he appreciated that she was still around the corner after she moved to a new team. He would make sure Nicole wouldn't be harmed on March 11.

Jeremy ate his cake, savoring every bite of chocolate that clung to the inside of his mouth, knowing it might be the last cake he ate for a long time.

The rest of the afternoon Jeremy spent cleaning up his email inbox and chatting with his friends. He had to fight off the thought of his friends possibly—likely—dying in a couple months, by his hand.

These are good people. But the experiment is bigger than them. It's their purpose. Their destiny.

He repeated these words to himself.

Three o'clock rolled around, and Jeremy had mentally checked out for the weekend, along with everyone else. He had just wrapped up his final scheduled call for the day and had an hour to burn when Shelly and Mark approached him at his desk.

"Hi there. Can we borrow you for a second?" Shelly asked. Whenever she greeted him in this manner, he knew it wasn't to chat about their weekend plans.

Jesus Christ.

"Sure." Mark and Shelly headed for the nearest conference room, and Jeremy followed them in. Shelly held a yellow folder underneath her arm that she placed on the table once everyone was seated.

Mark looked down at his fidgeting fingers, avoiding Jeremy's gaze.

Shelly spoke first. "I thought we were clear after our last talk, but apparently not."

"I'm sorry?" Jeremy had no idea what she meant.

"Do you still want to work here?"

Jeremy raised his eyebrows. "Yes. I'm very happy here."

"Then I suggest you start acting like it." Shelly opened the folder and pulled out two sheets of paper. "This is a PIP. We've decided to place you on one for the next thirty days."

What the fuck? PIP stood for Performance Improvement Plan, and they were given to struggling employees as a way to guide them back on track. It also made them ineligible for bonuses for the remainder of the quarter.

Shelly continued, despite the confusion on Jeremy's face. "Over the last couple months, your performance has been dipping. The quality scores on your calls are the worst on the team. As a team lead, you should be near the top."

That much was true. It was hard to do quality work when he didn't give a fuck.

"Also, I heard about your little conversation with Mark after the holiday party. Extremely inappropriate to tell your manager how he should manage his team. I'm including that on the PIP as well, to document your behavior. That kind of insubordination alone is grounds for termination, but Mark wants to give you a fair chance since you both had been drinking."

"Shelly, it really wasn't like that. It was a casual conversation. I wasn't trying to undermine Mark or anything like that."

"Regardless, it happened, and this is what we're doing about it."

Mark still hadn't looked Jeremy in the face. His eyes were

darting all around the room.

You slimy cocksucker. You set me up for this shit.

Jeremy should have known better than to get into a sticky discussion like that with his alcoholic manager. He'd gotten played. Played *hard.*

"And finally, your behavior today was the last straw. Mark went out and got you a cake for your birthday and when he came to deliver it to your desk and sing, you were nowhere in sight. No one on the team knew where you'd gone. You just vanished."

"What time was this?" Jeremy directed his question to Mark, who finally looked at him with weary eyes.

"Eleven."

"Oh, I just ran down the street to get some fluid for my car, don't think I was gone more than fifteen minutes."

"That's not the point. You can't just up and leave in the middle of the day. Lunch break, sure. After work, certainly. But at 11 a.m. you need to be accounted for."

Jeremy shook his head.

"Okay," he said. "So what happens now?"

"We will all sign this PIP, to commit to you getting back on track in the next thirty days. Now, I've done something different, since you've been with us for so long. I spoke with HR, and they have offered a package should you want to leave."

"A package?"

"Yes. It would be a check for a month's salary, and your benefits would run for two additional months at no charge to you. I want you to think long and hard over the weekend and let me know on Monday if you still want to work here. If not, the offer is on the table and there will be no hard feelings. I understand that we sometimes outgrow our place of employment. It's natural. Just think about where you fit into the big picture moving forward."

"Wow. Okay. I really have no intention of leaving, but I'll think it over."

"Mark, anything to add?" Shelly asked.

"Yes," Mark said, clearing his throat. "I'm here for you. If you don't want to leave, just let me know what you need."

"Thanks." He meant it sarcastically.

"Now let's sign this and get out of here for the weekend," Shelly said, scribbling her signature on the form before pushing it across to Jeremy. "You'll get a copy of this for your records, and a copy will be given to HR as well."

Jeremy signed and slid the paper back to Shelly. "Thanks. Sorry this all happened," he forced himself to say. *I should end you right now, once and for all. How dare you pull this shit on me.*

Shelly just stared at him, her face pale and lips pursed tight, then rose and walked out with Mark.

Jeremy stayed sitting at the table, dumbstruck. His mind raced, until he couldn't even grasp the thoughts he was trying to form.

"Do I move up the plan to the end of January?" he whispered to himself. "She can't keep doing this. I'm so sick of this shit."

No, you can't. Your PIP won't be over until February 6. If you do anything before then, you can kiss it all good-bye. No jury will believe that you didn't act out of revenge. It has to stay in March.

Thinking of his plan calmed him. Jeremy decided he would need to fight tooth and nail to keep his employment. Too much time, energy, and money had already been spent to let it all go down the drain. He couldn't believe all the bullshit he'd just had to sit and watch come out of Shelly's mouth—but he also knew that he needed to play her way and no other way. If Shelly asked Jeremy to jump off a bridge, he damn well better respond with "When and where?" if he wanted any chance of still being around in March. *I'm not sure what I did to piss her off, but that's irrelevant at this point.*

He felt dizzy as he walked out of the conference room, not speaking to any of his teammates as he gathered his things to head out for the weekend. *Shelly just tried to pay me to quit. Does she think she can buy my absence that easily?*

He would leave on his own terms, and she would know it when that day came.

33

February 8, 2016

The month following Jeremy's birthday was grueling. He had to try hard at his job, to maintain a high level of quality work. On top of that, he had to fake a perky and energetic persona to the rest of the team.

Despite not wanting to do it, it felt great to be needed again by his team. They came to Jeremy for everything, surpassing Mark in most cases.

He also made an effort to rebuild his relationships with Shelly and Mark, cracking jokes and keeping the mood light in team meetings. He had never realized how much work it took to do his team lead job well. The work week drained him like never before, making him feel slightly delirious by Friday afternoon.

When February 8 arrived, Jeremy went into his meeting with Shelly and Mark with his head held high. He knew he had succeeded and would be staying around a little longer.

Shelly closed the door and sat down. Mark looked at Jeremy with a wide grin.

"I'm so glad you decided to stay and work your way through this," Shelly said. "Your turnaround has been impressive. The old Jeremy is back and I'm so happy to see it." Her tone was light and pleasant, a 180 from their last conversation.

"So am I," Mark said. "I never knew the 'old Jeremy,' but seeing you work so hard lately has been a real treat. I look forward to working with you and helping this team grow."

"Thank you." Jeremy flushed at the praise. He never thought he'd receive so many kind words from these two dipshits. "I suppose I just needed that wake-up call. After so much heartbreak last year, it was hard to stay motivated. But I know what I want in life, and I need to be right here in this office." He laughed inside, knowing that wasn't a lie, but also was not the truth Mark and Shelly were hearing.

"I love hearing that," Shelly said. "We want you here. You have so much knowledge and are too valuable to the team." Jeremy knew it was all just an act. She had just tried to pay him off, and now couldn't stop gushing praise?

"What happens now?" Jeremy asked, ready to get the meeting over with.

"Well, nothing," Shelly said. "The PIP ends on today's date, as we agreed. Since we are satisfied with your performance, you just go back to normal. Let's just put all this behind us."

They all stood and walked out together, small talk flowing. Jeremy was amazed at how predictable it had all become. It felt like the same scene on a never-ending loop. Was that just how things went in corporate America?

34

February 26, 2016

Jeremy maintained his high level of work over his remaining weeks. From the time he was freed from his PIP he had exactly thirty-two days until show time. February went by in a breeze and March loomed.

Jeremy continued his training in the mountains, and by the end of the month was hitting the silhouetted man in the chest at least 70 percent of the time. He spread out more targets, on different trees at different distances. His performance improved so much that he no longer felt like he had to even aim. He could just whip King Kong in the direction he wanted and connect with every shot. It became second nature to shoot with accuracy and that excited him, giving him a high he had never felt before.

He felt ready in terms of the execution he would need to carry out on March 11, but he still needed to plan out the details for the day itself. There were plenty of matters to take into consideration, so he returned to the notebook.

March 11th
Time of attack?
8 am, 11 am, 2 pm
Keep King Kong in car?
Bring bad w/ loaded mags
How to lock doors?
Body armor?
Notebook?

Jeremy sat on his bed, notebook spread open between his crossed legs, and answered each question after thorough thought.

"When?" It was a question he hadn't asked before and it was an important one. Eight in the morning would be tricky as people would still be filing in for the morning. And not everyone started at exactly eight, so that was out.

"Eleven." Jeremy said it like a revelation. *Two can't work. Not on a Friday. A lot of people take half days on Friday and will be gone by two. Eleven is perfect. Everyone will be in, it's right before lunch.*

He circled 11 a.m. and grinned. It would also give him time for some last-minute schmoozing with everyone. In case there were any survivors, they could attest that Jeremy had acted normal, just like any other day, before he started blasting.

The notebook would have to be burned or disposed somewhere far away. Jeremy could drive an hour north of town and find a dumpster in a remote area. That would be less messy than dealing with its ashes.

"King Kong and my bag will be in the trunk. I'll go get it all at eleven." This seemed like an obvious detail, but he didn't want to assume anything and have a slip-up on the big day.

He had the magazines—he'd bought ten, which each held thirty rounds, online, with an alias, fake email address, and using a gift card that he had purchased in the grocery store with cash. There was no trail of his order that could easily be tied back to him. He'd even had it shipped to his office, to avoid his home address altogether. All he needed to buy now was the ammunition to fill those three hundred rounds.

Three hundred should be plenty. There's only 120 employees in the office. I can shoot everyone twice if I need to. He knew not everyone would be shot—especially the sales team, since they were on the second floor—but the higher the body count, the bigger the following the trial would have.

"Distraction and locking the doors," he whispered. A distraction could be anything from fireworks to a bomb—something to divert everyone's attention right before he started shooting. He wasn't sure what to use, and planned to come back to that detail.

As for locking the doors—that would be easy. All the exterior doors of the office building were double doors with pull handles. A long, solid object to run through the handles would be plenty, to keep the employees from opening the doors. One door would need to remain accessible, for him to enter the building with his rifle and bag. The main entrance would be best for that since it was the furthest door from where the shooting would occur, leaving his coworkers a difficult escape. The back and side door would have to be locked.

Smokers hung out near the back door, so once the coast was clear, he'd have to lock it and act fast before the next group of puffers decided to take a mid-morning break.

"Then what?" he asked. He flipped back to the map he had drawn of the office, and traced a path with his pen. If he entered from the main entrance, he could go into the office either through the lobby or through the side door in the hallway. The side door opened directly behind Shelly's desk, and he wanted to start there anyway. Logistically, he would be protected there, should someone try to make a move on him: his back to the wall and the rest of the department in front of him on the open floor. Shelly would be shot first; how everyone would react from that point on, he had no way of predicting. People would probably duck under their desks, others might make a run for the side exit, and maybe others would try to run across the office toward the front entrance. Would anyone try to attack him?

Jeremy pondered this, running through in his mind the seating chart of everyone in the office. Mark was certainly big enough to take him down if he wanted, but would he?

He decided it would be best to not leave it to chance: he would shoot Mark second. Mark's desk was only twenty feet from Shelly's, so it shouldn't be an issue. After that he would be showering bullets across the room. If people bottlenecked at the barricaded side exit, he would take them all out.

When he was done shooting, he needed to lay low before the police arrived. Drop his weapon and wait for the show to really begin. Once they arrived, he needed to act insane from that point forward. This part, he had given a lot of thought. He would remain silent unless spoken to, and then would only give short responses. He needed to seem distant, lost in his own mind, regardless of who he spoke to after his arrest.

Jeremy shook off the thought. That was getting too far ahead.

It's all done. I'm ready.

A final shooting practice would serve as a tune-up. He had learned to keep the images of his soon-to-be-dead coworkers out of his mind, numbing himself emotionally to the relationships he'd developed during his time at the company.

Jeremy cleared his mind of the thought. He always had a clear conscience when he laid down for bed each night and this night was no different. All he could think about while he dozed was that soon his life would change forever.

35

arch 6—Sunday

It snowed in the mountains, but not enough to keep Jeremy from driving to his final tune-up. Five days stood between him and his date with destiny, and his nerves were starting to work on his conscience. He still hadn't felt any guilt, still believed in what he was doing, but the enormity of his experiment was overwhelming.

He would be all over the news for weeks and months—maybe years, depending on how the legal process played out. Politicians would use him as an example of why guns needed better regulation, and doctors would use him as another reason mental health needed to be taken more seriously. The weight of the world bore down on his mind, heart, and soul. Did others before him feel the same in the days leading up to their history-changing event? Did Lee Harvey Oswald have doubts the week before he pulled the trigger? It was a lonely feeling, and he supposed he would need to get used to that. He would be in prison during his trial and, if things went right, a solitary ward at the mental asylum afterward. Loneliness was a sickening feeling.

Jeremy learned to clear his mind of all this shit when it came time to shooting. His thoughts were clear, and his aim true. He expected his final outing to be his best, and that was exactly what happened. Ten targets were arranged across the stand of trees, some near, some far. He hit each target with ease.

On his third reload, he hit each target twice within the same magazine. That was when he decided he was ready. Friday morning would be no different. His targets might move—but his hands moved faster, he was sure of that.

Jeremy fired his final practice round, a perfect head shot, then took a step back to inhale the clean mountain air. The smoky residue from the gun barrel filled his lungs, and he smiled. Nature had a way of reassuring him that everything would be alright. He packed up his rifle and left his uncle's cabin for the final time.

On his way home, he stopped at a gas station in Golden, roughly a half hour away from his apartment. The brisk air made him shiver when he stepped out of the car, causing the notebook to tremble in his hand. He stared at its black-and-white-freckled cover and brushed his fingers over it.

"So long, old friend. Thanks for helping me get this far."

Jeremy peered around to make sure no one was watching him, and dropped the notebook into a trash can next to the gas station's entrance. He drove off, looking into his rearview mirror as the trash can and gas station faded away.

"That's it," he said. "No more proof that this was all planned."

*****

March 7—Monday

Jeremy had hated Mondays since he was in high school, but this Monday was different. He had energy, and went into work perky for the day ahead. Knowing what was coming at the end of the week, Jeremy wanted to make sure to have closure with his closest friends at the office.

He and Clark went to lunch Monday, and as always it turned into a venting session.

"I'm so sick of Shelly's shit," Clark said. "It feels like it's some sort of game to her. I've worked with some incredible managers in the past, and she is by far the worst."

Jeremy nodded. "I know, man. Every day gets worse. You should start looking elsewhere. You and I both, for that matter. We have no future at this company."

They finished eating their burgers and headed back to the office. On the drive back, Clark said, "I'm really sorry for the way you've been treated. You should be managing a team somewhere in the company right now. The way she treated you really opened all of our eyes. If you're not immune to Shelly's wrath, then who is?"

"Thanks, Clark. I'm sure we'll both move on to better things soon enough."

Jeremy felt sick. He wanted so badly to tell Clark to take the day off Friday, but knew something like that would absolutely come back to bite him in the ass. If he could, he would just shoot Clark in the leg. If he had to choose one life to spare, it would be a toss-up between Clark and Nicole.

Just remember the big picture. Sometimes good people are lost for the greater good. If Clark doesn't make it, then just be sure he doesn't go in vain.

*****

March 8—Tuesday

Even though things had improved between Jeremy, Mark, and Shelly, she took one final jab at him before his final Friday.

The second week of March had always been performance reviews, and raises would be given based on the last year's performance. Jeremy would have planned his experiment a week earlier if he had remembered this detail, but it was too late for that now. He anticipated receiving a measly raise of maybe ten cents, but what happened caught him off guard and cast doubt on his plans.

"I really am glad to see the improvement you've made since your PIP," Shelly said to start off his review. "It's encouraging and we're excited. However, today's review is based on your last year of performance, and since you were on a PIP, we're not going to be able to increase your pay at this time."

Jeremy's stomach sunk. Shooting his two managers the same week they stiffed him on a raise wouldn't look good.

How he responded now would be critical. If word leaked back to the HR department that Jeremy looked even a little bit upset, that could be held against him.

"Okay, fair enough." He swallowed his pride. His leg started to bounce.

"Since you've been such a good sport about everything, I did arrange with HR for us to have another review with you in September. If you keep up the way you are I don't see any reason to hold back a raise for you then."

"Thank you, Shelly, that's awesome of you to do." Jeremy bowed his head toward her in gratification. *Too bad you'll be nothing but rotting bones come September.*

Shelly gave a genuine smile, and Jeremy knew he had succeeded with his positive reaction. If she had anything to report to HR it would be minor and positive.

Three more days stood between Jeremy and his experiment. He could feel the universe pushing, not wanting him to carry out his plans, but he chalked it up as subconscious guilt.

I'm home-free. This bullshit was my final test, and I passed. No looking back now.

*****

March 9—Wednesday

The workday dragged, and so did Jeremy. He had a rough night of sleep, tossing and turning until two in the morning. The thought of his upcoming actions on Friday weighed heavily on his mind, and for the first time he felt intimidated by the size of his task.

No matter how hard he tried to separate his conscience from the situation, he felt guilty about the potential of killing those he had grown so close to. When he arrived to the office with bloodshot eyes, Sylvia noticed and brought him a coffee. Without that, he likely would have fallen asleep at his desk before nine.

He fought his way through his morning calls before surrendering at lunch to take a nap in his car. He set his alarm for one hour, reclined his seat, and fell asleep on the warm March afternoon.

The power nap was all he needed. When he woke, the throbbing in his head had left, his eyes no longer felt puffy, and he felt he could make it through the rest of the day. He had dinner planned with his parents later that evening and would need to power through a little longer than normal.

Fortunately, the afternoon was slow. Jeremy had two calls on his schedule and none after three, leaving him the last hour of the day to hang out.

He spent his time at Sylvia's desk, catching up, hearing about how her son was doing in school and football, before the conversation took a turn. Sylvia looked around and whispered.

"Did you hear about Janae?" she asked.

"What now?"

"Nothing work-related for once. But she was fucking Kevin

over the weekend." Kevin worked in the sales department upstairs, after having left the service department a few months prior.

"Oh? Well, I know Kevin gets around a bit. Can't say I'm surprised."

"I know. Guess I shouldn't be shocked either that Janae is a ho."

"Well, when you gotta suck your way to the top, what do you expect?"

Sylvia chuckled. Jeremy looked over the desk divider and saw Janae sitting at her desk. His heart sunk. She looked occupied in her work, but the office was quiet enough for her to have overheard the entire conversation if she was paying attention.

Jeremy made a slashing gesture with his hand in front of his mouth, and Sylvia understood to end the conversation right away.

Fuck.

Jeremy returned to his desk and continued the conversation over the chat system.

Do you think she heard? he typed.

I hope not...I don't think so, Sylvia responded.

Well, let's just hang low. We can talk about this at lunch tomorrow.

Ok cool.

Jeremy wrapped up for the day before heading out. "Bye, Janae," he said on his way out.

"Have a good night!" she said, not showing any signs of anger. Jeremy assumed she must have not heard and sighed in relief.

He left the office for his parents' house across town in Larkwood. He had planned a final dinner with them, knowing it could be the last one for a very long time.

When he arrived an hour later, he could smell the spaghetti and freshly baked bread oozing from the open front door. His childhood home was a small ranch-style house with an extended driveway that reached to the backyard. Jeremy parked behind his dad's car and headed up the short three steps to the front door.

He opened the screen door and stepped in to find his dad on the couch, drinking a beer and watching basketball.

"Lakers look like shit this year," Robert Heston said. "Oh, well, guess they had a good run."

Robert took off his glasses to rub his eyes and scratched his graying head. Lately work had started to take its toll on him, draining him of energy by the time he came home.

"How are things with you, son?"

"Not too bad. Just working and keeping busy."

"Still no promotion?"

The topic of work made Jeremy uneasy, especially since he had finally managed to clear his mind of what he needed to do on Friday morning. His body flooded with sorrow at the thought of this being the last time he'd be dining with his parents.

"Not yet, hopefully soon. Things are starting to come together, so we'll see."

"I thought I heard you!" Jeremy's mother, Arlene, exclaimed as she came around the corner from the kitchen. "Dinner's almost ready. I made your favorite."

"I know. I could smell it from outside. Can't wait." Jeremy spoke with relief, thankful his mom had come in to change the subject.

"You look skinny," she said. "Are you eating enough?"

227

"Yes, Mom. I had a bad cold not too long ago, might have lost some weight then."

"Okay, good. Let's set up the table, guys."

Jeremy followed his mom into the kitchen, where the smell of the bread warmed his soul. He started putting out plates and silverware and Robert joined them in the dining room. With everything set, Arlene brought over the heavy bowl of spaghetti for serving. The bread was wrapped up in a bowl on the center of the table.

The reunited family ate their spaghetti, sharing stories of what had been going on in their lives. Arlene was ready to retire from her elementary teaching job after thirty-five years, while Robert knew he had at least five more years of dragging himself to the office before he could call it quits.

"Are you seeing anyone?" Arlene asked Jeremy nonchalantly.

"Not right now. Just trying to work on myself and get my ducks in a row. I just feel like I don't know what I want to do in life anymore."

"Welcome to being in your twenties," Robert said while he struggled to twirl noodles around his fork.

"I'm sure you'll figure it all out," Arlene said. "At least you're almost done with school. That should be exciting, right?"

"Yep, two more months and I'm free."

Jeremy felt suddenly nauseous. He wanted to tell his parents. All they'd ever done was love him and raise him to be a good person. They wouldn't see the purpose of his experiment; they'd think their only child had turned into a monster. What would their friends and the rest of the family say? He knew his actions would have horrible consequences for his parents that they simply didn't deserve. They could be shunned by the rest of the family, forced to move away from the lives they had built.

Then again, isn't the point to affect as many people as possible? His family and friends would also be sucked into the drama of Jeremy's story, regardless of how it ended.

He still felt like a balloon had inflated inside his gut. He couldn't even look at his spaghetti.

Arlene sensed his sudden mood shift. "Are you sure you're okay?" she asked him. Robert remained oblivious as always, consumed by the delicious meal in front of him.

"Yes, sorry. I'm still not feeling a hundred percent. Think I just need a good night's sleep. Haven't been getting as much as I should."

"Well, let's pack up some dinner and you can take it home. You need your rest. You have a long two months coming up before graduation. You need to be healthy."

You have no idea.

"Thanks, Mom, that sounds great." Jeremy didn't want to leave his parents so abruptly, but he thought if he stayed any longer the guilt would make his head explode.

Arlene packed up two containers of spaghetti for Jeremy to take home. She would see those same containers in Jeremy's refrigerator, untouched, a week later.

Jeremy was feeling worse by the second. He hugged his mom and dad. "I love you guys. I hope you know that."

"Of course we do, Jer Bear. We love you too." Arlene squeezed him tight as Robert put his arms around both of them. "Now go get some rest."

"Thanks, Mom."

Jeremy returned to his car and pulled out of the driveway.

After turning off the street he had grown up on, Jeremy cried the whole way home.

*****

March 10—Thursday

Jeremy arrived at work feeling rested and somewhat clear-headed. Crying had lulled him into a much-needed deep sleep. His eyes felt swollen and puffy, but at least they weren't red. No one at the office could tell that he'd cried for two hours straight the night before, as he started to question his own sanity.

He didn't want any more emotional outbreaks on the eve of the big day, so he spent his morning hard at work, avoiding conversations with those around him. Sylvia sent him a chat to see if he was okay, but he ignored it. He just wanted to get through the day and go home to make his final preparations.

His emotions were all mixed up. Sorrow, anxiety, and sickness spiraled around, his thoughts chaotic. Every time he stood up from his desk, he couldn't help envisioning what the office would look like in twenty-four hours: blood and bodies scattered across the floor. The casings from his spent rounds. Him sitting among his dead coworkers, waiting for the police to arrive and take him into custody.

Jeremy shook the images from his mind, focusing on getting through the day ahead. He managed to stay busy enough to avoid talking to anyone before lunch, and took his lunch break away from the office. He was hungry, having not finished his dinner the night before and skipped breakfast. It was also his last day of freedom, so he decided to splurge a little.

He went to the burger joint across the street from the office, and ordered a double bacon cheeseburger with a rum and Coke and their legendary garlic fries.

Not bad considering it'll be jail food for a while.

He ate his burger in peace, until he saw the highlights on the TV above him of the game his dad had been watching the prior night. Seeing it took him back to his parents' house and he fought off the tickling urge of tears that welled up behind his eyeballs.

His lunch ruined, he forced down the rest of the meal, left a twenty on the table, and headed back to the office. His plan for the rest of the afternoon was the same as the morning: sit down and grind away at work until it was time to go home.

He was able to do that, for the most part. At one point, Sylvia walked around to Clark's desk. He was certain they were talking about him, but he kept his focus.

2:45. Almost there.

But he wasn't. Shelly came over to his desk at 3, tight-lipped and not looking pleased.

"Let's go have a talk," she said.

What the fuck is it now?

Shelly turned and walked toward the conference room. Mark joined her and Jeremy followed them into the room. She didn't wait for Jeremy to sit before speaking.

"This is the last straw," she said, not bothering to sit, instead propping her hands on the back of the chair facing Jeremy. She spoke down to him, and Jeremy didn't like that. "I don't even know what to say to you right now."

"You can let me know what this is about, because I have no idea." Jeremy spoke confidently, but calmly.

"You and Sylvia talking shit about Janae right in front of her."

She paused. Mark nodded his head silently, and Jeremy waited for her to continue, but she didn't, and his heart sunk into his stomach.

"Sylvia called me over to her desk then just started talking. I had no idea where it was going."

"Save it. We've been through this. You have to take ownership for your mistakes. If Sylvia started it, you should have ended it, and you didn't. You stood by and let it happen. The things you two were saying—it's flat-out bullying. Despicable."

"I'm sorry. I should have been more aware." Jeremy felt his heart racing, sensing every detail of his planning about to come crashing down. *Fucking Janae. Just stay calm, just get through this day and it can all end tomorrow as planned.*

"No more apologies." Shelly crossed her arms. "I'm thinking about firing you. You've become such a cancer to our team. It may be time for us to go our separate ways."

"I think that's a bit drastic," Jeremy said with a slight tremor in his voice. The nerves flooded his entire body and the world started to spin around him.

"Well, that's how I feel. You should think long and hard about what happens next." Shelly walked out of the room with Mark.

Jeremy did exactly as Shelly had said. He went home and thought about what was going to happen next.
*****

Jeremy paced around his apartment, sweating and shaking. *This isn't fucking happening. This is not fucking happening.*

He could end up fired from his job on the morning he was supposed to carry out a mass shooting to change the face of mental health. The mere thought of Shelly burned a fire so deep within he felt like going to her house and stabbing her on the spot.

"She goes first tomorrow. And there *will* be a tomorrow, because I'm not fucking getting fired. I didn't come all this way for nothing. This is destiny." Jeremy spoke rapidly, under his breath. "Tomorrow is happening if it's the last thing I do."

He stormed into his walk-in closet, throwing clothes all over the room until he had his hands on what he needed. He clenched a black long-sleeved hoodie in a tight fist and took it out of the closet.

"You're fucking done tomorrow, Shelly Williams."

Jeremy opened his rifle case, which lay on the floor of his bedroom, and pulled out King Kong, throwing it on his bed.

"The best way to get acquitted is to give them a show. Everyone loves a good show."

Jeremy grabbed his phone and King Kong, and positioned the barrel of his rifle just below his chin. He opened the camera on his phone and started taking selfies of himself posing with King Kong. The camera snapped and clicked numerous times. In some pictures he smiled, in others he kept a serious face, and in one he stuck his tongue out at the camera.

His logic was to leave a trail that he had lost his mind and was appearing crazy on the night before he gunned down his office. He finished his photo shoot feeling satisfied and ready. Thinking about Shelly only further committed him to his plans for the next day.

"How dare you call me a bully. I'll show you a goddamn bully."

Jeremy packed his duffel bag, placing his black hoodie in first, followed by the loaded magazines. King Kong was returned to his case, and Jeremy took everything out to his car trunk.

"Tomorrow's the big day. Time to rock and fucking roll." Jeremy knew he wouldn't sleep—he could feel the adrenaline flooding his veins. He popped two sleeping pills and lay in bed. It wasn't even eight o'clock yet, but his angst was too strong to attempt any sort of task. The night would pass and tomorrow would arrive. The wait would finally be over.

36

arch 11—Friday

M The sun was unforgiving, brightening Jeremy's room like a photography studio. Regardless, he slept until his alarm sounded at seven sharp.

His guts bubbled out of control. The nerves had built up even more while he slept. He tried to shit out the nerves, but had no luck.

With everything ready in his car, Jeremy only had to get dressed and ready for the day. He dressed in his normal work attire: jeans and a T-shirt. His hair had grown long, and he combed it back to tuck under a hat. He knew he should eat breakfast, but his appetite had vanished.

"Time to roll." He spoke into his living room, scanning the room for anything he might want to take with him. Nothing important stood out, so he turned off all the lights, closed the blinds, and walked out to his car, knowing it might be the last time he ever did.

The warmth of the day swarmed him. The forecast called for an eighty-degree day and not a cloud in the sky. In early March, it felt like a summer day, even though snow would be coming on Monday. Birds chirped in the tall trees standing above the apartment complex. Jeremy felt in tune with all of his senses, not wanting to take anything for granted on what could be his last day of freedom, or the last day of his life.

He had put on a crucifix necklace his grandmother had given him before she passed away. If things went wrong, and he wound up dead at the end of the day, he needed as much peace as he could get.

During his drive to the office, a small stretch of the route faced the Rocky Mountains straight on. They looked majestic with their soft blue tint in the distance, and the snow-capped tops were like something out of an artist's painting.

"They really are beautiful." He drove in silence; no music, no talk shows. Just himself and nature one last time. Friday mornings were always light on traffic, and Jeremy arrived to the office at 7:45.

He parked in front of the side exit doors so he could have a more central station when the time came to get things ready. Sylvia's car was parked across the lot, and he knew she would have questions for him. It was never a secret when someone on the floor was pulled into a meeting room. Everyone would sneak a peek, to try and get a read on both Shelly's and the employee's faces. The way their meeting had ended yesterday was sure to be causing a buzz around the office.

Since he didn't see Shelly's car yet, he figured he would go inside and get the awkward conversation with Sylvia out of the way. He wouldn't tell her that he might be getting fired, but she should be aware of what they'd talked about, since it involved her.

Jeremy grabbed his backpack that he always brought to work and entered through the side doors he would be barricading in a few hours. He strolled across the floor, nodding to a couple of support team staff on the way to his desk. Sylvia met him at his desk as soon as he arrived.

"Everything okay?" she asked.

"Yeah. Why?"

"You've been acting weird the last couple days. Then your meeting with Shelly yesterday didn't exactly look like a happy discussion."

Jeremy nodded. "We were overheard the other day." Sylvia stared at him, confused. "Janae heard it all and ratted on us."

"That fucking slut." Sylvia's expression changed from puzzled to furious in the blink of an eye. "What did she say?"

"I don't know exactly what she told Shelly, but she knows we were talking shit, and that you called her a slut. Shelly called us bullies."

"Did Mark say anything?"

"Of course not. He sat there quiet and useless like always."

Sylvia grunted in disgust. "So does that mean I'm getting talked to today?"

"I'd assume so, so be prepared to try and bullshit your way through it. Not that Shelly will hear any of it. Whatever Saint Janae says goes, there's no reason to hear anyone else's side of the story."

Sylvia shook her head. "They on some bullshit around here, Jer. I can't do this shit anymore."

She went back to her desk and banged on her keyboard while continuing to shake her head. They wouldn't speak to each other for the remainder of the morning.

*****

Jeremy made his eight o'clock call and managed to make it take up an entire hour. When he wrapped up the call at nine, he noticed Shelly had still not arrived to the office. This was concerning, since she was usually in before eight.

Is she coming in today?

Mark had shown up on time and avoided Jeremy at all costs.

He was flustered by Shelly's absence. The purpose of his experiment was to bring the issue of mental illness into the limelight, but the biggest perk was the opportunity to blast that two-faced bitch in the head. He considered calling it all off if she didn't show up.

But then what? Get fired today and have a clear motivation if I come back and try later?

It had to happen today, and it had to happen at the originally planned time of eleven if he wanted to execute it before his job was terminated.

He returned to his desk with a glass of water, and Clark came by to greet him.

"Hey man, everything okay? You were pretty out of it yesterday."

"Yeah, was just trying to hit my numbers. Sorry if I've been distant."

"It's cool. Gotta stay under the radar these days. I get it."

"Indeed."

"Alright then, sir, I'll leave you to it. Almost free for the weekend. Have a good day." Clark left Jeremy to return to his desk without another word. Jeremy thought back on that conversation vividly, remembering those were the last words Clark ever spoke to him.

Jeremy had a 9:30 call to make, which would be his last work call ever. The thought of that liberated him.

He glanced around the office. *Live or die today, one thing is certain. I won't be coming back to this fucking place again.* He dialed his final call, and completed it as smoothly as ever.

*****

He was writing his notes for the call at 10:05 when Shelly

walked in. The sight of her brought relief and a new, different kind of stress. She strolled by the onboarding team, gave a quick grin to Mark, and proceeded to her desk without acknowledging anyone else on the team. Her tired face suggested a long night, possibly of contemplation about him.

Janae spoke in her high-pitched voice, and the sound made Jeremy's blood boil. *That bitch threw me and Sylvia under the bus.* If he could avoid Shelly for the next fifty minutes he'd be in the clear, so he went to the bathroom to sit in a stall and gather himself.

He sat down on the toilet and buried his face in his hands. *This is it. It's actually time to change the world. Never thought this day would come.*

Jeremy's legs shook and bounced to the point that he had to push down on them to make them stay still. The feeling of impending doom consumed him, and his emotions turned numb. He interlocked his fingers in prayer.

"God, please forgive me for what I'm about to do. My intentions are pure. Remember me how I was before today." He whispered in the stall, not wanting to be overheard by anyone coming in for their morning shit. One last flood of tears remained in his ducts, and Jeremy let them flow. It was a silent cry, no sniffling or sobbing, just tears falling from his face to the floor in a miniature puddle.

He checked his phone and the clock read 10:35. Jeremy stood from the toilet and took a deep inhale, feeling at peace with his soul.

It's time. Everything is in place. No need to wait another half hour to get started.

*****

The sunlight blinded Jeremy when he stepped out the back door exit. The parking lot was deadly silent and the sea of cars glared at him. No smokers were around, further confirming his decision to get the party started sooner. He walked around the corner of the building to his car, and went straight to the trunk, which he opened with the remote.

The duffel bag and rifle case were neatly aligned. He pulled the black hoodie over his tee. Only the flesh of his face and hands showed, and he reduced this too, by putting on sunglasses that hid everything from his forehead down to his nose.

Jeremy grabbed the duffel bag and slung it over his shoulder. The bag probably weighed twenty pounds with all the ammo stored inside, but his adrenaline was starting to pump so hard it felt like a little kid's backpack. He felt like his hands were moving faster than his mind could process as he watched them open the case and pull out King Kong, smacking in a magazine in the smooth way he had perfected over the past few weeks, and pulling the rifle's strap over his other shoulder.

Time to hustle. Jeremy had planned a minute in total to get from his car to the back door, barricade it, run around to the side door, barricade it, and run to the front door of the building, to enter the office from the inside door behind Shelly's desk.

He'd bought a couple of two-by-fours from the hardware store to stick between the door handles. He grabbed them and broke into a sprint for the back door of the building. The glare of the sunlight off the reflective glass zoomed by as he ran.

To his delight, the back door remained deserted. He fed the wood between the handles and pulled on them to test it. The doors opened a couple of inches before hitting the wood, which wouldn't budge. *Perfect.* He pivoted and broke into another sprint, like a baseball player trying to steal second base.

When he rounded the corner toward the side door, he skidded to a halt when he saw Clark walking out of the building. He didn't notice Jeremy and kept walking to the back of the parking lot, where he always parked. *I guess it's your lucky day, Clark. Good for you.* As long as Clark stayed outside until the firing began, he would make it home to his wife and kid.

Jeremy returned to running when Clark disappeared into the parking lot. He placed the block of wood between the side door's handles, and wasted no time sprinting for the front entrance. He knew anything, in the next few seconds, could change the outcome drastically. The main entrance was the one variable he couldn't predict. Anyone could walk in or out at any time.

Jeremy pulled open the doors, and as he stepped in a man dressed in an all-black suit walked toward him, to exit the building. He thought about shooting him, but the man—who had pale skin and black, slicked-back hair—winked at him as they passed each other in the doorway. The man's leg bumped the duffel bag and Jeremy felt the hairs on the back of his neck stiffen.

The brief encounter cost Jeremy a handful of seconds, but he pushed forward down the hallway, where he could see someone approaching the back door. He stopped in front of the door that would open to Shelly's back, pulled King Kong around to get a grip on the gun beneath his sweating palms, and pulled open the door.

The office looked the same as always. Everyone sat or stood at their desks, either typing on their keyboard or talking on their phone. Normally music blared on Fridays, but no one had turned the music on yet, so the room felt quieter than normal, almost still. The door clicked shut behind him, but no one paid him any attention.

King Kong was cocked and ready, safety turned off, as he positioned the butt into his shoulder. Instantly, he felt the sensation of the gun becoming an extension of his arm. When he had that feeling, his aim never failed. The adrenaline tried to burst out of his fingertips, pulsing desperately against the cool steel of the gun. Even his eyeballs pulsed as his vision focused in and out. Despite that, his hands remained still and confident.

He stood five steps behind Shelly, her back to him. He took soft steps toward her and tapped the tip of the rifle on her shoulder. "Hey, cunt."

"Excuse-—" *BOOM!*

Jeremy pulled the trigger as soon as she turned her head. The shot echoed throughout the quiet office and blood and brain matter splattered across ceiling, computer screen, and desk, as her body collapsed to the floor, knees thudding first.

Instantly all eyes were on him. "What the fuck?" someone shouted from the back of the office.

Mark sat fifteen feet from Shelly's desk, on the end of his team's island. He looked at Jeremy in confusion, trying to figure out who was behind the sunglasses and black hoodie.

Jeremy swung King Kong around to aim at Mark and pulled the trigger again, without hesitation. The slug caught him in the chest, where a dark pool of blood immediately formed on his light blue shirt. Mark grasped at the spot on his chest as his mouth hung open, gasping for air.

Two for two. It had felt like five minutes, when in reality it had only been fifteen seconds.

His shot accuracy as sharp as could be, Jeremy started swinging King Kong from person to person, pulling the trigger with the ease of flicking on a light switch over and over. Green chunks from the desk dividers blasted in every direction with each shot he took.

Screams broke out. Some people ran frantically around like headless chickens and others took cover under their desks.

"Everybody get the fuck out!" someone screamed. "He's got a gun!"

"Oh, my God!"

"Help!"

Jeremy felt his mind numb as he emptied the first magazine. He watched through his eyes while his hands and trigger finger did all the work.

He replaced the magazine with a fresh one with a quick flick of his wrist. A group of maybe six people huddled near the side exit, banging on the door.

"It's not opening. It's fucking locked!"

Pop. Pop. Pop. Pop. Pop. Pop. Pop. Pop. Pop. Pop.

He reloaded again and pulled the trigger, watching each body at the door fall to the ground into a limp pile. The sound was repetitive and flat, each shot echoing around the office walls as the screams faded towards silence.

He scanned the room and saw bodies splayed across the office floor, splatters and actual puddles of blood on the carpet. A head poked around the corner near the side exit, and Jeremy whipped the rifle over and fired. He was sure it was one of the girls from the HR team.

The office was silent now, nothing but the steady hum of computers. Jeremy had changed magazines three times, meaning he had fired at least ninety rounds in less than two minutes.

He had two more magazines in the duffel bag and planned on using them, so he crept toward the corner, where Miss Human Resources had just been, and saw all of Nicole's team absent. They'd likely run out the front door of the office, he thought, but then he saw that the training room on his right was full of sales team members that must have come down for a meeting. They had turned the lights off inside the room, but with the light from the office Jeremy could see at least ten people hiding under the desks.

The more, the merrier! The higher the body count, the more attention I'll get.

He pulled open the door and walked to the front of the room, facing the desks. "Class is in session, motherfuckers."

More screams broke out in hysteria.

"Don't do it!"

"PLEEEEASE!"

Jeremy fired more rounds. The barrel of the gun started heating up, but Jeremy didn't notice, numb to everything happening outside of his mind. He had one more magazine to use, but nothing left to shoot, so he walked calmly back to his team's side of the floor and looked for Janae.

He wanted to make sure Janae wasn't getting off easy, like always. He found her on the ground, lying next to Cherie below their desks. Cherie had her eyes closed and a pool of blood underneath her back, making her purple hair look black instead. Janae had been hit and lay on her side, blood pouring from her mouth and stomach, shivering in a pool of her own blood.

"This is kind of your fault," he said to her, no emotion in his voice. "I hope it hurts."

Her brown eyes gazed at him, and her lips quivered. Jeremy assumed she was trying to speak, but couldn't. He stepped around her to get on the other side of the island, where Sylvia lay splayed on the floor, a clear gunshot wound in her throat. Her eyes stared lifelessly at the ceiling.

"I'm sorry, Sylvia. I promise this won't be for nothing." Jeremy ran his eyes over her eyelids to close them.

He saw Elayna on the opposite side of his desk. He could see a wound in her leg and blood puddling beneath her, but she lay still, likely playing dead. A quick mental estimate suggested he had shot at least forty people in all, so he decided to show some mercy on Elayna.

Police sirens sounded in the distance.

"Now the hard part begins. May we all be a special part of history. You'll never be forgotten."

Jeremy sat in his desk chair, dropped King Kong to the floor, and waited in the silent office for the next three minutes, until the S.W.AT. team arrived.

37

Epilogue

"Denver PD! If you have a weapon, drop it!" a voice barked as the doors burst open from the side exit. Five S.W.A.T. team members entered the room, guns cocked and aimed, looking for anything suspicious. Bodies lay all over the room, except for Jeremy, who stood from his desk with his hands raised above his head.

"Don't you fucking move another step!" the man screamed, and Jeremy froze.

Three of the men dashed for Jeremy and tackled him to the ground, securing handcuffs around his wrists in seconds.

"Bag his hands!" the one who arrested him shouted. "He's got powder on his hands."

Someone pulled tight, plastic evidence bags over Jeremy's hands. Knowing he needed to appear as insane from this moment forward, he started to make puppet gestures with the bags behind his back.

"How are you, Mr. Bags?" he asked in a low voice, opening and closing his right hand in a speaking gesture.

"It's a delightful afternoon, wouldn't you say?" he responded with his left hand.

The man who had cuffed him stood in shock as he looked around the room. He pulled his radio from his shoulder to his lips. "I need every officer and ambulance I can get right now. There's bodies everywhere." He spoke calmly, probably in disbelief.

More S.W.A.T. entered the building, breaking off into different directions. They would find a surprise in the training room, but everywhere else had been left untouched.

The arresting officer read Jeremy his Miranda rights. "Do you understand your rights?"

Jeremy grinned and nodded.

It felt like at least an hour that Jeremy kneeled in the middle of his office with his hands cuffed behind him. He kept staring at King Kong, resting on the floor, lifeless and innocent without his touch. As word started to reach the public about what had happened, cell phones started ringing all around the office. Buzzing and ringtones created a mix of chaos, until they hauled Jeremy out of the office.

They took him out of the side exit, and he caught a glimpse of his car, which hadn't been touched. A couple of news vans had already arrived on the scene and caught Jeremy being pushed head first into the back seat of a police car.

It was a short ride to the police station—six minutes, he had calculated—and the driving officer didn't say one word. Meanwhile, the radio cut in and out, with other officers screaming at the scene Jeremy had left behind.

"There's fucking blood everywhere! There's at least fifteen bodies that I'm counting. No one touch the bodies, leave everything how it is until forensics gets out here. We need more officers. There are survivors that need to get to the hospital!"

Jeremy grinned in the backseat. He had accomplished what he needed to. Fifteen dead was plenty to get national attention.

*****

Jeremy's arrival at the police station was greeted with more camera crews and chaos. The officer pulled up to the back of the building, but the reporters ran around back, in an attempt to get footage. The officer pulled Jeremy out of the car and was able to get him inside before the cameras could catch a glimpse. He guided Jeremy straight to a holding cell. *Damn. Wish the world could have seen me before they took my clothes and threw me in a jumpsuit.*

"We need to get blood work right away from him. Let's see what kind of drugs he's on," another officer said.

The holding cell was roughly the size of the living room in his now-abandoned apartment. The walls were solid white with no windows, and the door of bars had clanked shut.

The next hour brought many visitors in and out of the cell. Some doctors, both medical and psychiatrists, came in. The medical ones poked him with needles, took his blood, and checked his body for injuries. Psychiatrists asked him if he knew his name and his current location. He responded with a blank stare and silence.

At one point a forensics specialist came, removed the bags from his hands, and swabbed them.

Finally an officer came in and uncuffed his hands. "Heston. You're gonna be here over the weekend. Your first court date is Monday. You will sleep, eat, and shit in this room until then." The pudgy man had a bald head and a slight northeastern accent, but Jeremy couldn't pinpoint from where exactly. He walked out of the cell without another word. *I never told anyone my name, but they know. The plan is ready.*

Jeremy would sit alone in that cell for the next forty-eight hours and change. Officers came in and out of the station, poking their heads into his cell to get a look at him. Most had likely come straight from the office; blood soaked their clothes and skin.

A stocky Latino officer limped over, and Jeremy noticed a terrifying scar that ran across his cheek. "I hope you burn in hell for this," he said in a raspy voice. Before the officer turned, Jeremy caught his last name, Lopez, from the badge on his chest.

He lay down on his cot, staring at the ceiling, hearing the roar of the press outside each time the doors opened. A TV blared in the background, and the reporters spoke in serious tones about the dozens of people killed and injured. Flustered survivors gave interviews about the banging sounds they had heard underneath them and the chaos of being trapped in the building.

Must be salespeople. Don't recognize any voices.

Jeremy wasn't tired, but he closed his eyes. The day was still young, word was still making its way across the country, but everything was officially in motion.

You did it. A grueling legal process now awaited him. Monday would be day one, and he needed to appear every bit as insane as he could sell. The initial hearings would be described by broadcasters, but he fully expected his actual trial to be televised.

Part one is done. The experiment begins.

Jeremy kept a certain thought in his mind as he started to doze, reassuring himself that this experiment would be a long and drawn-out process.

Good things come to those who wait.

Acknowledgements

I owe a huge thank you to my editor, Teja Watson. This story was complex to tell and she helped me get it where it needed to be as an easy read. Her contributions to this book are truly invaluable. I'd also like to thank my aunts, Chris, Tanya, and Maria for being early readers and providing feedback to ensure the book was as strong as it could be. Last but not least, my incredibly supportive wife, Natasha. She always makes sure I'm moving forward and has been the biggest help on the business side of my writing habit. Thank you to everyone that made this possible, I can't wait to get the final two books out!

As I mentioned in the dedication, I was fortunate to survive the Aurora theater shooting that took place in July 2012. That day was a big wake up call for me to start chasing my dreams, and every time I write I have those who weren't able to make it home, in my heart. A dozen lives were taken, all with long futures ahead. Don't be afraid to chase what you really want in life, because tomorrow really is not a guarantee.

Andre Gonzalez
September 20, 2017

Thank You

Thank you for taking the time to read my work. As an independent author, receiving reviews are critical to any future success. If you enjoyed the book (or even if you didn't), I ask you to please leave it a review. You can leave reviews on Amazon or Goodreads. This will help me not only with promoting this current work, but future books as well. I appreciate you taking the time if you choose to do so!

I also look forward to connecting with my readers to discuss this book, or any book, for that matter. If you have not done so already, feel free to follow me on my social media sites and subscribe to my mailing list through my website!

www.andregonzalez.net
Facebook: www.facebook.com/AndreGonzalezAuthor
Twitter: @monitoo408
Instagram: @monitoo408
Goodreads: www.goodreads.com/AndreGonzalez

I'm always open to any discussion surrounding my work and would love to hear your thoughts!

Made in the USA
Columbia, SC
09 December 2018